# LINDSAY

# LINDSAY

## A Woman of Courage

## Joanne Ryan

VANTAGE PRESS
New York

To everyone who cared

# LINDSAY

# Chapter 1

All night long, Lindsay and her children sat glued to Channel 5 watching the severe weather bulletins. It was their first ice storm in a new city, far away from family and friends. The move to Atlanta from Hudson, Ohio, was to be Mark's big chance in the corporate world. The telecommunication industry was the latest scientific explosion, and Mark had been actively recruited because of his exceptional background. The move was the promise of a new start for not only the advancement of Mark but for Lindsay and Mark's marriage. In Hudson, the gap between them had widened, and Mark and Lindsay both wanted to save what they had, or so Lindsay thought.

The children were already celebrating the impending school closing and had put all thoughts of studying out of their mind. The fireplace blazed and sputtered with the freshly cut pine logs that Mark had insisted on ordering before he left for San Francisco. How could Lindsay doubt Mark's caring and love for the family? Hadn't he always provided the very best for them? Thoughts like this kept Lindsay from really seeing the other side of Mark; the side that sometimes forgot about his family and marital fidelity.

The call that Mark had promised to make was hours late, and Lindsay was beginning to get uneasy with old doubts and thoughts. Where was he? Why didn't he call or return her calls? Damn him. She had been calling his hotel room since eight o'clock at night, and now it was after three in the morning. Where was he?

The storm grew closer, and Lindsay kept checking the phone to make sure the lines were still working between calls to Mark's hotel room. She was glad that the children had fallen asleep; she did not want them to hear her on the phone.

"Operator, please make sure you have the right Summerfield."

"Mrs. Summerfield, I have checked with the front desk, and I have the right room; he just isn't answering." She was beginning to sound frustrated. Lindsay wondered how many times she had called. She figured this had to be around the tenth or fifteenth call. She knew deep down that she couldn't produce what didn't exist. Mark had played his disappearing act again and no one would be able to find him until he chose to be found.

"Please send up the hotel security officer to see if he's all right." Lindsay knew that the operator would do this just to satisfy her and get her off the line for awhile. The operator agreed, and Lindsay waited on hold for what seemed like an eternity. Finally the operator came back on the line.

"Mrs. Summerfield, we had the security officer check Mr. Summerfield's room, and he is definitely not in his room. Do you want to leave another message, or are the previous ones sufficient?"

"Thank you for all your trouble. I don't think there is a need for another message. I won't be bothering you again this evening." The operator just hung up, without even a good-bye; Lindsay didn't blame her.

She hung up the phone and went into the bathroom to get a glass of water, when she caught sight of herself in the mirror. Dark circles under her eyes glared back from the mirror. Why did Lindsay do this to herself? Most women would never put themselves through this agony to find out the truth. They would just pretend that it wasn't happening.

Crawling back into the bed, wondering whose bed Mark was in and with whom didn't help to relax Lindsay's mind enough to fall asleep. The satin sheets felt smooth and cool next to her skin. Looking across the wide expanse of the king-sized, four-poster bed made her feel so alone and vulnerable. What if Mark decides to never come home? Could she live without him? The bay window in the bedroom was covered with ice, and beads of rain made splashing noises against the panes. The coldness of the ice and rain brought shivers to Lindsay's body, and she decided to take off the flimsy black nightgown and put on one of her old flannel nightgowns. Digging through the storage area of the closet, she came across the old, worn flannel nightgown that she kept from college. Feeling its comfort and warmth, she went down to the kitchen to make a cup of tea. The tea kettle was slow to boil, and as Lindsay waited, she checked on the latest weather bulletin on the cable weather channel.

Atlanta was definitely socked in for at least the next twenty-four hours. Banking a fresh supply of logs was out of the question, as snow and ice drifts were piled high in back of the door. Matt would have to go around the side of the house to get the logs in the morning.

Taking the cup of tea up the circular staircase to her room, Lindsay suddenly felt at peace with the situation. There really wasn't anything she could do to make things happen; perhaps they would get better on their own.

Sitting on the window seat with her favorite afghan that her grandmother made as a shower gift, Lindsay thought back to when she had first met Mark. No matter how angry she would be with him, she always affectionately remembered that first meeting.

Lindsay was a junior in college, and a group of her friends were invited to a mixer at a boys' college; it was at a private club in town. She was with her steady boyfriend, Scott, who had come home from Dartmouth for the holidays.

Scott, as usual, had found some friends to chat with and left Lindsay to sit and wait for him to return. She guessed it must have been fate that brought Mark into her life that night, as Lindsay was definitely not looking for someone else. She felt a tap on her shoulder, and when she turned around, there stood a great-looking guy. His blue eyes and blond hair looked striking against his tan face.

"Hi. I'm Mark Summerfield from Carroll, and I would like to ask you to dance."

"Really?" It was all Lindsay could say.

"Sure, you're the prettiest girl here. I've been watching you since you came in."

Blushing, Lindsay nodded yes, and they walked onto the dance floor. She caught the profile of Scott engaged in conversation with his friends, unaware of what Lindsay was doing or with whom.

"So tell me. What's your major? Where do you go to school?"

Lindsay quickly mentioned her school and what her major was. They made small talk until the music stopped. Thinking that she should be returning to the table to wait for Scott, Lindsay turned to leave the dance floor.

Suddenly Mark grabbed her arm and said, "No, you don't. I'm not letting you get away."

Lindsay was back in Mark's arms, in a slow dance to the song, "Moon River." This time there was no conversation, just slow, sensual dancing. Mark's arms pressed Lindsay's body to his; each move was more sensual than the one before. Only their breathing could be heard above the music.

Lindsay never did return to Scott that night, as she and

Mark quickly slipped out of the club into Mark's parked car. They had barely gotten into the car when Mark's mouth was on hers. His arms were holding her body tightly. The radio was playing romantic music, and Lindsay wished that the night would never end. The windows were steamed with fog from their heavy breathing. Pushing Mark away, Lindsay realized that this was happening too fast.

"Mark, I think I had better go in and tell Scott that I won't be going home with him."

Opening the door to his Ford convertible with one hand and fastening her blouse with the other, Lindsay walked back to the dance. The party was thinning out, and she didn't recognize anyone from her group. It was obvious that Scott had left and probably would never speak to her again. She had humiliated him in front of his friends.

Lindsay walked into the restroom to refresh her makeup and comb her hair. She couldn't go home looking as if she had been necking all night. Her face was flushed with a rosy glow that she had never noticed before when she had been with Scott. This was a new feeling that she couldn't put her finger on. What was happening to her? The nuns had never told her about this feeling.

Upon closing the door to the restroom, Lindsay saw Mark waiting for her.

"How about a ride home?"

Smiling, Lindsay walked arm in arm with Mark to his car. The ride home was filled with tenderness as Mark held her hand and told her his life story. Each word he spoke tugged at her heart. His father had died when he was nine. He was the eldest of four. He had put himself through Catholic high school and had earned a scholarship to college.

Lindsay's heart poured out to Mark as she thought of her affluent upbringing. Suddenly, the cashmere sweater that she had on made her feel guilty for what she had. Even though she had not met his mother, she immediately was angry with her for neglecting Mark. How could a mother make her son work so hard so she could be a social butterfly?

Lindsay's parents were asleep when Mark walked to the door with Lindsay. Tomorrow would be soon enough to tell them about Scott and Mark. Standing on the front porch with the street light shining on them, they kissed good night.

"I'll call you tomorrow after I get off of work."

Mark had a part-time job at a gas station near his college several days a week in addition to working at the college. Lindsay thought that she had never felt so wonderful in her life.

Quietly, Lindsay climbed the steps to her bedroom, hoping that no one was up so that she could just lay in bed and remember the night with Mark. The down comforter had been pulled down and her nightgown was placed across her pillow. The full moon filled her room with light as she undressed and crawled into bed. Tomorrow couldn't come soon enough for Lindsay as she waited for Mark's call.

Waiting had always been the magic word when it came to Mark. Sitting on the window seat with her tea cup, she quickly put the past out of her mind. The past memories would cloud her mind, and she would not see things as they really were in the harshness of the dawn light.

Feeling totally exhausted, Lindsay decided to lie down; there was absolutely nothing she could do until the storm was over. She was trapped by the storm and thinking about Mark. She didn't remember pulling up the covers as sleep finally let her mind rest.

# Chapter 2

Lindsay woke to the sound of icicles crashing against the window panes. Fierce winds howled through the air ducts in the attic crawl space above her bedroom. She knew by the severity of the wind that the storm had knocked out the power lines, even before she looked at the electric clock on her bedside table. Looking at the clock, she saw the electricity had gone out around 5:38 A.M. The diamond watch that Mark had given Lindsay for her birthday showed the time to be 7:42 A.M. Luckily, the furnace had been out only a short time; and the house was just beginning to chill from the lack of heat. If she hurried, maybe she could at least start a fire in the living room, where they had put in gas logs because of the white carpet.

Lindsay pulled on a pair of Mark's hunting socks and his heavy corduroy bathrobe and rushed down the stairs to the living room to light the gas logs before the children woke up. At least they could all have cold cereal and Pop-Tarts until the heat came on and the electric stove would be in operating condition. Guilt swept through her as she looked around at their beautiful home. Mark had let Lindsay have a free hand in both the decorating and purchasing of the furniture. If nothing else, they were a great working team. Mark knew Lindsay's taste as well as she knew his. Sitting in one of the matching white armchairs, she could smell Mark's scent in his robe; she missed his arms around her.

The fire was just beginning to warm the living room, when the phone rang in the family room. Lindsay knew before she picked up the phone, it was Mark with a very convincing tale that would sound so logical that even she would be ashamed of herself for ever doubting his loyalty and love for her. Before Lindsay reached the phone, it stopped ringing; someone else had picked up the phone.

She carefully picked up the phone and heard Megan's voice on it. Lindsay heard Megan sounding so excited, saying to her dad, "You should see all the snow and ice. When are you coming home to be with us? It was so scary last night with the wind howling and the pine trees bending almost in half." Dear Megan, her father's pride and joy from the moment he saw her in the nursery. Megan saw only how much she loved him, not Mark's imperfections that others saw and that she and Lindsay chose not to see.

She pictured Megan curled up under the Laura Ashley rosebud comforter, in her pink flannel nightgown, talking on her white princess phone. Mark and Megan had chosen the furniture and wallpaper for her new room so that the transition from Hudson to Atlanta would be less painful. Mark thought that everything that money could buy would make the loss of friends and family easier for her, but nothing was further from the truth.

The small talk continued about the storm, Matt, Jennifer, and Mark, Jr. "Is your mom around?" Finally he was getting to Lindsay. She quickly put the phone down, hoping that no one noticed the click. Picking up the phone, Lindsay sounded glad to hear from him.

"Hi, honey, I'm glad you called. I really miss you."

"Miss you too, sweetie. I can't wait to get home and curl up by the fireplace with you. I know that it has been a drag without heat and electricity, so if it is better tomorrow, we'll go to Chequers for dinner."

No mention of the phone messages or where he had been all night, but there was the peace offering, dinner for just the two of them.

The electricity came back on just as she hung up the phone, and she finally brewed a fresh cup of coffee. Relaxing for the first time in what seemed like forever, she realized how very tired she was. She took her cup of coffee upstairs, turned on the Jacuzzi tub, and added fragrant bath oil to the water. This was Lindsay's favorite room in the house. Mark and Lindsay had designed the house down to the last brick on the front walk. The stained glass window depicting the Peaceful Valley by Tiffany was in the center of the bay window over the Jacuzzi tub. How they had laughed over thoughts of candle light and wine while they were in the Jacuzzi tub together. Thinking back now, Lindsay had been the only one to use the tub, as Mark was always in a hurry and showered.

Lindsay poured bath oil into the tub, undressed, and climbed in. Instead of wine, she had her cup of coffee on the ledge. The sun's rays cast beautiful streams of light over the carpet and walls. The stained glass window was so beautiful and picturesque that she wanted just to lie and soak all day in the tub. For now, she wanted only to forget about the night before; she hoped that she had been wrong in her suspicions. She sometimes wondered what would really make her leave Mark. Infidelity was on the rampage, one knew just by picking up any magazine or listening to talk shows on television. It was all the topic of conversation. The statistics of a second marriage succeeding were practically zero, from what she had read, let alone seen among friends; she wished with all her heart that she could be like the women she knew who saw and heard nothing, all the while putting money aside in a secret account. She knew that no matter what she felt like doing, she could never be dishonest and lie to Mark.

The expensive bath oil made the water feel like silk against her skin. Lindsay wondered if Mark would even notice how well she tried to take care of herself for him. Years ago she had read an article on Jackie Kennedy's daily skin regimen and had followed her advice. She was not foolish enough not to realize that the finest skin products, manicures, massages, and facials go a long way in keeping the aging process at bay.

Lindsay thought about what she would wear this evening when Mark arrived home. Not knowing for sure what time that would be, she decided on a soft velour, two-piece lounge outfit in deep burgundy with a satin ribbon trim at the neck and cuffs. Looking through her lingerie drawer, she decided to wear her newest Victoria's Secret satin bra and panties in a soft shade of eggshell, with lace and satin at the waistband of the bikini panties. Patting Carolina Herrera after-bath lotion on her naked, damp body, she thought how wonderful it would be if Mark were here to massage the lotion over her body. Maybe she would suggest a body massage later this evening after the children were in bed.

With thoughts of Mark's homecoming in mind, Lindsay carefully dressed and applied her makeup before tidying up the bedroom. She placed scented candles on the night table on Mark's side of the bed and changed the satin sheets and sprayed perfume on the sheets and pillowcases. Tonight would be a night for Mark to remember for a long time. Until she found out whether there was someone else, she would try her best to make this marriage work.

The time dragged until Lindsay thought she would scream if she didn't hear Mark at the door soon. The children had gone to the mall with friends, and the house was so quiet that the ticking of the grandfather clock could be heard throughout the house. She heard the sound of the car door slamming before she heard Mark at the door. Her heart pounded with excitement as she threw open the front door and ran into Mark's arms.

Mark's smile was all she needed to tell her that she was wrong to have doubted his love for her. "Honey, I really missed you." His arms held Lindsay tightly to his body, so tightly that she could feel his heart beating against her chest.

"Mark, I love you so much and miss you terribly when you're away." She didn't want to break the spell by moving even an inch. Safe and secure in Mark's arms, all questions and suspicions from the night before vanished from her mind. Lindsay thought, *He's here, he's mine and no one will ever take him away from me.*

"Lindsay, you smell so wonderful. New perfume? I really like it. God, I'm so lucky to have you." The words just melted her heart and all she craved was Mark.

Lindsay and Mark climbed the stairs together. "Where are the kids?" Mark asked.

"They went to the mall with some friends."

"Great. Let's take a nap. You remember our first time together?"

Yes, Lindsay remembered, and no amount of time could make her forget that wonderful night so many years ago. Each time Mark took her into his arms was as exciting as the first time, even after all these years.

Guilt swept over Lindsay as Mark took her into his arms. Was this the action of a man involved in an affair? Mark's clothes were lying all over the floor; he was so anxious to get into bed that he had forgotten about closing the door to the bedroom.

"Mark, I have to close the door. What if one of the children comes home and we don't hear?" Gently she moved Mark's arm from her hip and got up to close the door. She walked back to the bed, and Mark reached up to pull her down to him.

"Have I told you recently how very much I love you? If not, I want to tell you now." Mark smiled and nuzzled his lips against her ear as he spoke. His lips met Lindsay's, and all the love they had for each other poured forth.

Later that afternoon as they lay together under the down comforter, they spoke of their feelings for each other. Lindsay looked into his beautiful blue eyes and wondered if perhaps her obsession with him had clouded her judgment. Looking into his eyes, she asked the question she needed to know. "Mark, would you ever leave me for another woman?"

Looking totally shocked, Mark raised himself on his elbow to get a better look at her face when he spoke.

"Lindsay, I can't believe that you would ever think that. You know how much our religion means to me. I stood before God and took our marriage vows. Remember that line 'until death do us part'? I certainly do, and you had better also or one day you will have to be accountable before God."

A shiver went through her spine at the intensity of his words. She knew better than to ever broach that subject again with Mark. She would just have to have faith in his word.

Lindsay lay in Mark's arms wondering if she had been mistaken in her thoughts last night or if she had married the biggest con man there was. Watching Mark's sleeping face, Lindsay wondered which it was. Thoughts of last night slowly started to creep through her mind. Soon the American Express bill would be arriving and she could track the trip to San Francisco through it. One of these days, Mark will get smart and have all his charges sent to the office. Then she would have no way of knowing anything. Lindsay heard the children open the door; she quickly got up and dressed and went down to see what they had purchased with their fun money.

The kitchen table was covered with bags and paper cups from McDonald's.

"Wow, you guys must have bought out the store."

Megan just laughed and pulled out a crazy T-shirt. "Don't you just love it?"

Megan was dancing around the kitchen, holding up the shirt and swaying to the music on the stereo.

Mark wouldn't be asleep long with all this noise. Matt just looked disgusted and went out to the garage to polish the MGB. Lindsay wished that she could make his stay here happier than it was. The boy across the street had forgotten to pick him up for the party on the Friday night before, and he had been so depressed since then.

Jennifer just sat there pouting, as she couldn't find anything to fit her that she liked.

"Mom, I wish we could just go to Country Blues, where they have everything I like."

Lindsay knew that there was a lot of comfort that she missed from that small town, where all knew the Summerfield children so well that they were able to sign their names to any purchase from Saywell's drug store to Mary and Ted's restaurant. Hearing Mark's snoring upstairs, Lindsay hoped that all this unhappiness to further Mark's career would not be wasted on a cheating husband and father.

# Chapter 3

Saturday night dinner at Chequers was lovely. Mark and Lindsay arrived around 8:00 P.M. for cocktails and dinner. The small combo was playing soft fifties music, and memories of days gone by were ever present while they danced before dinner arrived at their table. The notes of "Moon River" made Mark whisper in Lindsay's ear, "That's our song, remember?" How could she forget? That dance and song had changed her life forever. Instead of thinking of Mark, her mind wandered back to Scott, the boy she had been with that fateful night so long ago.

Scott had been at Lindsay's door early the next morning to take her to mass at Saint Anne's. If he was upset, he didn't act it until they were in the car and away from the house. Instead of driving to church, Scott pulled into Shaker Lakes' parking lot. Shaker Lakes was noted for a convenient place to neck, away from the eyes of parents. Scott hadn't said a word in all the time it took for them to drive from Lindsay's house to the lake.

When he turned off the engine, he turned and faced Lindsay, looking directly into her eyes. For the first time, she could see the hurt in his eyes, and she felt so guilty that she quickly looked away. What had she done to hurt such a great guy, she thought. Scott took her hand in his, and all the old comfortable feelings came back. Still, they did not compare to the sensual ones that she had felt with Mark. She knew right then that no one could make her feel like Mark did, and he was all she wanted forever.

Scott asked what had happened the night before in a soft, loving voice.

"I'm so sorry, Scott; it just happened. I wasn't looking for anyone else, honestly. Maybe we had been drifting apart for months and I didn't know it because we have always been so comfortable with each other."

"Lindsay, honey, you are making a big mistake. I can forget about last night. I just don't want to lose you to Mark, of all people."

"What's wrong with Mark? What do you know about him that I don't?"

"Lindsay, that guy comes from a really screwed up family. I checked. He doesn't even see his mother when she comes to Carroll to visit him. Come on, if you're going to leave me for someone, pick someone better than me." Anger built up inside Lindsay, and without thinking, she slapped Scott as hard as she could.

"Don't ever talk about Mark like that. He is better than you, and I want you to take me right home or I'll walk."

The ride home was so silent that Lindsay could hear the ice crunching under the tires as they drove. Scott never said another word to her, and she often wanted to get in touch with him to apologize for slapping him. She never did talk to him after that; maybe someday she would.

"Hey, where is your mind? The music has been over for a few minutes and you are a million miles away in thought. A penny for your thoughts."

Lindsay smiled up at Mark, turned, and they walked to their table just as the waiter appeared with their salads. He must have been watching for them to stop dancing before serving.

Dinner was wonderful, and the music put both of them in a wonderful mood. Driving home, Lindsay cuddled next to Mark, enjoying the music on the radio and Mark's company. The children were asleep when they arrived home. Mark and Lindsay climbed the stairs together and checked on the children. Nothing made Lindsay happier than seeing the children safe in their beds. Her thoughts of Mark, Jr. were the most heartbreaking at this time of night. Although they talked regularly on the phone, she never ceased to wonder if he was all right and well fed. Lindsay made a mental note to call him in the morning.

If it was possible, the night before paled in comparison to this night of love. Mark was so tender and complimentary that Lindsay wondered again how she could mistrust him. They finally fell asleep around dawn, exhausted and deliriously happy. Maybe Lindsay was on her honeymoon again; no, it was better this time.

Mark awoke around nine, and he and Lindsay decided to go to ten o'clock mass together. Then they would go to Coco's for breakfast. The children wanted to sleep in, but they promised to go to the five-thirty mass that evening.

Sitting next to Mark and waiting for the priest to start mass, Lindsay glanced over at Mark, who was kneeling in prayer. Mark wouldn't walk in church and receive communion if he had sinned, would he? No one could possibly know that answer except Mark and God. Lindsay had to leave that thought alone or she would drive herself crazy.

After breakfast at Coco's, Mark wanted to drive up to the mountains. He had read an interesting article on a mountain community called Big Canoe Resort. It was such a beautiful day that Lindsay was eager to take a ride, and of course be alone with Mark. Big Canoe was a good hour's ride from

Atlanta. By the time they reached the resort, Lindsay was so relaxed and happy with her life that anything that Mark wanted to do would be fine with her. They took the tour and then went to the Chimney's restaurant for lunch.

The restaurant was beautifully done in Williamsburg blue and off-white walls. The corner fireplace was paneled in pecan wood and dental trim. Lunch was delicious, and Lindsay was famished after walking through the lots that were for sale. Lindsay and Mark had narrowed down their selection to one beautiful lot in the estate section, close to the community center and golf club. The front of the property looked over the championship golf course, and the rear of the property had a magnificent view of the mountains and a narrow stream, babbling in the distance. The street name was Wilderness Parkway, and it suited the area perfectly.

After signing the purchase agreement and having another glass of tea with the salesman, Lindsay and Mark decided to take another look at the property before returning to Atlanta. A slight drizzle had started, and in the car, surrounded by beautiful trees and pines, Mark had a wonderful idea.

"Let's look around and buy a lot for each of the children. It'll be an investment towards their future."

"Mark, what a wonderful idea. I can just picture our own little compound in the mountains with our grandchildren swimming and boating all summer long."

They both elaborated on the fun the children would have with their own little mountain cabin.

"Lindsay, let's stop at the chapel for a minute before we start home; I hear it's beautiful."

They say ignorance is bliss; what an understatement. Nothing could have prepared her for what she was to hear. The chapel was absolutely beautiful in unadorned decor. Brass chandeliers hung from the ceiling, and at the back of the altar were three tall cathedral windows of varying height. The dark burgundy carpeting against the oak paneling and off-white walls intensified the greenery of the pines and dogwoods outside. Taking Mark's hand in hers, Lindsay suggested that they renew their wedding vows on their anniversary, in July.

"I'll pick a time when all the children could be here and my parents, too."

Mark just put his arms around her and held her body tightly to his. The rain had turned into a thunderstorm with lightning and thunder. The sky had become as dark as night, and an eerie feeling came over the chapel.

"Lindsay, I have something to tell you, and I don't want you to overreact when I do. You know how much I love you and the children."

What was he trying to say? Was he ill? Was he in trouble?

"Mark, you know that you can share anything with me. What is it?"

"Lindsay, as much as you say that, I know that it will be difficult for you to understand what I'm about to tell you."

Tears were running down his cheeks and a chill shook her body. This was going to be serious, Lindsay knew in her heart.

After a few minutes of silence, neither of them were talking; they just looked at each other. Mark put his hand into his pocket and pulled out a small bottle of white pills and handed them to Lindsay. The name on the pharmacy was unknown to her, until she looked at the address of the pharmacy, San Francisco.

"What are the pills for, Mark?"

Mark just sat there silently, staring at the altar. Tears began streaming down his face. This was more than a slight problem, so Lindsay questioned further. Getting no answer, she just sat there and played the waiting game.

Finally, Mark spoke, avoiding Lindsay's eyes.

"Honey, I really don't know how to tell you this, but you are going to have to see a doctor, soon. I've contracted a disease, and you have to be checked as soon as possible."

The floor came up to meet Lindsay, and she felt hot and nauseated at the same time. Why now? A cold chill now replaced the heat flash, and Lindsay trembled all over uncontrollably. She could feel the tears rolling down her cheeks and into her lap.

"Lindsay, say something. Please don't cry. Lindsay, please don't leave me."

They sat in silence, neither one of them knowing what to do next. It was as if Lindsay's world no longer existed as it had.

"How did this happen, Mark? You promised that you would never get involved again. I trusted you, and took you at your word. Is your word so worthless that you can't have any morals or principles? I moved my children and left Mark, Jr. behind to satisfy your career, and this is how you repay us?"

Mark just sat there, staring straight ahead, silent.

Finally Mark turned to Lindsay and tried to put his arms around her waist, as if to hold her from running away.

"Lindsay, stop crying. I'm sorry. I can't tell you how terribly sorry I am. Nothing means more to me than you and the children."

Getting no response from Lindsay except for hysterical crying, Mark found the one area that she would protect at all costs, the children.

"Please don't react this way or the children will know. How could they take the changes that they have been through with an unfaithful father to deal with at the same time? Do you want to scar them for life?"

Mark was now totally in remorse, cradling his face in his hands. His sobbing could be heard throughout the chapel. Was this the same man who had gone to communion this morning and made love to Lindsay last night?

Think of the children. That was always Mark's answer to any confrontation that would disrupt his lifestyle. Yes, Lindsay would think of the children, above and before herself, as she always had. Never would she intentionally hurt her children. Lindsay knew that telling them would be crossing the line of no return for them. Tomorrow she would call her doctor and take whatever steps she needed to physically get through this. She waited outside the chapel while Mark made peace with God. They drove home in silence, the joy of the weekend gone forever.

# Chapter 4

All night, Lindsay was awake, wondering how Mark could have cheated on her. Mark went to sleep without a word, only looks of regret and worry on his face. Yes, this was something that couldn't be swept under the table and forgotten. Listening to his breathing, Lindsay wondered who she was and what she had that Lindsay didn't have to offer Mark.

When Lindsay had called for an appointment, Sally, the receptionist, had tried to schedule an appointment for two weeks from the next day; they were booked until then. Lindsay told her that she had a medical emergency and that she had to see Dr. Houser the next day. As usual, Sally tried to screen the emergency to see how important it was to see the doctor early. Lindsay told her that it was personal and she needed to talk to the doctor first. Finally, Sally agreed and gave Lindsay a one o'clock appointment.

The ride to the doctor's office was done in silence. Mark's other woman was on Lindsay's mind to the point that she could think of nothing else. What did she think of Mark? How could she pass along an infectious disease and not care? Lindsay knew little about this type of disease, but she hoped that she had found out about it early.

As Lindsay and Mark walked into the waiting room, Lindsay felt all eyes on her. Sally seemed to brush Lindsay off as she signed her name. Lindsay was sure that Dr. Houser was not happy with an extra appointment, having such a busy schedule.

The waiting area was full with pregnant women, and thoughts of her own pregnancies came back to Lindsay. She felt so alone, even though Mark was sitting next to her, reading a magazine. Memories of Mark and her in the obstetrician's office waiting for each checkup came back. Mark had been so full of love and caring. Lindsay wanted those memories to replace the ones that she would remember now forever.

Finally, Lindsay was called into the examination room, and the nurse asked her why she was there. Lindsay asked the nurse to have Dr. Houser speak to Mark in his office before he came in to see Lindsay. The request seemed to surprise her, and she just stood there for a moment, as if she didn't know what to do next. It seemed like an eternity before the nurse came back and asked Lindsay to take off her clothes from the waist down and lie on her stomach. The nurse never looked into Lindsay's eyes as she spoke.

The rap at the door announced Dr. Houser's entrance.

"Lindsay, Mark has explained everything to me. I'm going to give you an injection in each buttock; then you should be fine."

It was probably Lindsay's imagination, but she felt as if the doctor wanted this over more than she did. She stared at the wall in front of her, noticing every hairline crack. The shots were over before she had the time to wonder what to say or do next.

"I'll be back in, and we'll talk for a minute."

Dr. Houser walked out of the room, and Lindsay struggled to sit up and get dressed. Every ounce of strength had left her body, and she felt as if it would never return. Was

Mark worth all this? Did the vows for better or worse mean this?

Another rap at the door, and Dr. Houser sat down on the stool in front of Lindsay. Neither of them spoke for a few minutes, and then he cleared his throat and told her the complications of the medicine he had injected.

"Lindsay, all men make mistakes; Mark is no different. But if his infidelity continues, I would suggest you see this psychiatrist." Lindsay took the card and looked at it through tear-filled eyes.

She thanked the doctor and walked out of the office to where Mark was waiting. She handed Mark the card, and they walked to the car.

Driving home, Mark tried to make small talk, but Lindsay just nodded or didn't say anything. Maybe they should see someone who was equipped enough to handle these matters. Lindsay was open to it, but was Mark? Mark stopped at a red light and reached over for Lindsay's hand.

"Lindsay, please understand that it isn't your fault. It is me. Four children in four years, all the moving, and now this. I am sure that I have broken your heart, and that is something that I never want to lose. I want us to grow old together."

So did Lindsay, more than Mark knew.

"Mark, I am going to call the psychiatrist that Dr. Houser recommended, and we are going to get some counseling." Lindsay's voice was firm, and her eyes never wandered from Mark's. She meant what she said, and he knew it.

They pulled into the driveway just as the kids got off the bus. Mark walked up to meet them, and Lindsay rushed inside to wash her face and freshen up before they saw her. She could hear happy voices drifting up the staircase, and she knew that no matter how she felt about their father's indiscretions, she would never want them to know.

"Mom, Dad is taking us to Coco's for dinner; he said to

hurry up." Coco's was the kids' favorite restaurant in Atlanta. It was a family restaurant and many of their school friends went there with their families.

The car ride was very lively, as each of the children had some new tale to tell about school. Mark looked over and winked at Lindsay. Maybe the children were finally adjusting to their new school. The saying "time takes care of everything" may be true.

Lindsay could barely swallow her food, as the memories of the last forty-eight hours kept returning Mark didn't seem to have a care in the world as he laughed, joked, and ate.

As the Summerfield family was finishing dessert, Mark looked at Lindsay and said, "Lindsay, why don't you go over to Rich's tomorrow and buy that oriental rug you've been looking at."

Lindsay's fork froze in midair. So this was the peace offering for the infidelity and social disease that he had brought to their marriage.

"Mark, I believe that we have an appointment to make before I go to Rich's."

Mark's facial muscles twitched, and Lindsay knew he was angry. Well, so was she! Tomorrow she would start taking care of herself, no matter what steps she had to take.

As soon as the children left for school and Mark left for work, Lindsay dialed the number on the card. A receptionist answered the phone.

"Dr. Moorehouse's office. . . . I'm sorry, but Dr. Moorehouse is going to be away for a month's sabbatical until July 26. I can give you and your husband an appointment at three then."

Lindsay agreed to wait until then and hung up the phone. She quickly dialed Mark's private number, and he answered.

"Mark, I made an appointment with Dr. Moorehouse for us on July 26 at three. Please put it into your daytimer."
"Great, I'll do just that."

# Chapter 5

Matt was stomping around the kitchen, slamming cupboard doors and acting as if he had just lost his best friend.

"Matt, what's wrong?" Lindsay could tell that he had had another miserable day at school.

"You know what's wrong. It's that lousy school, that's what's wrong. No one wants to sit with me at lunch, and the teachers suck. What more can be wrong than that?"

Trying to collect her thoughts, Lindsay went into the laundry room to fold some towels. Why did she need this now? Hadn't the weekend been a disaster? Walking back into the kitchen, Lindsay found Matt talking on the phone to his brother Mark, Jr.

"Mark, you should see these creeps. They just think they're everything. You know what they would do to them in Hudson." At least he knew that his brother would understand and not give him the cold treatment. "Mark, and another thing: Dad is traveling more than ever. Remember how he promised that this new job would keep him home more? Well, it isn't. Same old garbage all the time. Lies, lies, lies. That's all he knows."

Lindsay reached for the phone to talk to Mark.

"Hi, honey. Sorry that Matt upset you. You know that

it's difficult for all of us and especially me. I have to hear all of it."

Mark just listened and said that it would work out. Dear Mark was so kind and good, always thinking of the best in people.

"What's this I hear that Dad is still on the road? I thought that was over with."

"It's his job, whether we like it or not. You know that we have four of you to get through college."

Matt started screaming that he would put himself through college and that he wanted out of here.

"Mom, just let him get it out of his system, and he'll be fine."

Sure, Lindsay thought. If she didn't go crazy first.

"I'm planning on coming down for a week soon, and we'll get through this together. Now, don't worry."

Hanging up the phone, Lindsay wondered when she would have nothing to worry about.

Hearing Matt go up the stairs to his bedroom, Lindsay walked out on the deck and looked at the beautiful pink dogwood that was in bloom. Atlanta was truly a beautiful city; the houses that were being built were each more spectacular than the other. Except for a few homes that Lindsay had seen in Hudson, everything paled in comparison to Atlanta homes. If only Sherman hadn't burned down Atlanta, the beautiful antebellum homes would be a treasure to own. Mark would certainly have liked to own one and reconstruct it. Mark, with all his faults, liked to have beautiful things for his family. This house could attest to that.

Matt was upstairs talking to himself again, and Lindsay knew that she would have to leave him alone; there was nothing she could say or do to help see him through this. Only time would help.

Finally, Matt came downstairs and sat next to his mother on the glider.

"Mom, just tell me. Why do we do this for him? I just want to know."

"Honey, this new job is going to do a lot for Dad and us. You know that he said everything would be better here for us; we have to believe him." Lindsay tried to sound convincing, but when their eyes met, she knew that they both knew better; Lindsay looked away. How do you tell a sixteen-year-old that his dad really wants the best for him, but didn't have the will power to be faithful to his wife or children?

Jennifer and Megan came downstairs and wandered onto the deck; they sat across from Matt and Lindsay. Megan was the first to speak.

"Matt, Dad is trying, and you have to give him a chance. Jennifer and I don't like Dunwoody High School either. You know that all the girls wear high-heels to school and dresses. We just wear our Lee corduroys and rugby shirts. Talk about not fitting in." Jennifer just kept nodding as Megan spoke.

Silence was so thick that you could have cut it with a knife. Everyone was deciding what strategy they would take to survive this. At the same time, Mark was at his challenging job, enjoying the perks of the upward mobile executive. He was so unaware of all that was happening at home. Yes. In the end, the Summerfield family would support Mark and be behind him a hundred percent. Mark's family was his strongest ally.

Tonight would be a night that Mark would walk through the door and never know that his family was suffering emotionally because of him. He would only see four happy faces waiting for him to come home. Dinner talk, pleasant and stimulating, filled with happy stories of the day. No one would let Mark down and tell him that all he was doing for his family was not enough to make the pain go away.

That night, lying in bed next to Mark, Lindsay thought of the past week. She had been checked by a doctor, informed of another woman who was thousands of miles away, and the rug was on order. Only the appointment with the psychiatrist was still lurking in the darkness. Lindsay had called a few medical friends, and they had assured her that Dr. Moorehouse was very good in marital counseling. Reassurance was all that Lindsay needed now, as she felt threatened in every way. The children had readjusted and were sound asleep in their beds, waiting for all this to be a memory.

From the sound of Mark's breathing, he was sound asleep, completely contented with his life. Lindsay once asked him how he could just put his family out of his mind and pursue other women. He just looked at her and shrugged his shoulders, unwilling to talk about it. Lindsay knew that it was painful for Mark to admit his infidelity, even to himself. The one and only time that he mentioned anything to her had been in the chapel; he never mentioned it again after that.

Not feeling sleepy, Lindsay got up and walked downstairs. She sat on the glider on the deck. Remembering the photo album that Rebecca had given her of Mark's childhood, Lindsay thought of the pictures that were in the album. The beautiful blond baby boy, who never had a smile on his face, always looked sad. Even then, he was a loner. Later, Lindsay would hear stories of how Rebecca had kept Mark locked in his bedroom, watching him through a glass door as he played by himself. As a mother herself, the thought of locking a baby behind a glass door was unthinkable to Lindsay. She had never trusted Rebecca with her own children for fear of what she might do to them.

Thinking of Rebecca brought back the memories of the

first time Lindsay went to Toledo to meet Mark's parents and family. Lindsay was unaware of the strange relationship that Mark and Rebecca had until she arrived that very cold and snowy December night in Toledo. Mark was waiting at the airport for Lindsay, and as she walked off the plane, he was standing there with a beautiful bouquet of roses in his arms.

Instead of going directly to Mark's home, they went to a party in the "old west end" of Toledo. The homes were large and gracious and beautifully decorated for Christmas. Mark obviously was very popular and was warmly received at the party. Lindsay was the girl that Mark had told his friends about; he was proud of how she looked that night in her wool, camel's hair suit from a specialty store in Cleveland. The party was wonderful, and Lindsay liked all of Mark's friends.

On their way home to Mark's house, they discussed who would be at their wedding and what kind of wedding it would be. Lindsay was so happy, her insides trembled with feelings of love for Mark that she could still remember after all these years.

Mark's mother and stepfather were waiting up for Lindsay and Mark when they arrived late that night. Rebecca wore a beautiful royal blue velvet jumpsuit with a pearl necklace that matched the pearl bracelet on her right arm. Not a hair was out of place as she sat like a queen on a stunning wing chair by the roaring fireplace. Her right hand cradled a cut-glass goblet filled with wine. She rose to greet Lindsay and flowed across the floor.

"Lindsay, welcome to our home. We have heard so much about you from Mark that I feel like I know you already." Leaning down to hug her, Lindsay smelled Chanel. Sidney, the stepfather, also hugged Lindsay and welcomed her into their home, They looked so mismatched in appearance that Lindsay would never have placed the two together.

Sidney was shorter than Rebecca and not as polished. It was apparent that he worshipped Rebecca and couldn't keep his hands off her.

Mark brought in Lindsay's matching set of luggage and showed her to her room in the rear of the house. The bedroom was beautiful with a four-poster, black walnut bed with a canopy. The wallpaper and drapes were in a Schumacher print of pinks, greens, and yellows. Kissing good night was very hard for both of them, as neither wanted to leave the other.

"Lindsay, someday soon, we'll never have to leave each other at night again. Remember that, it will make things easier now." Lindsay just nodded, not quite understanding the strange powerful feelings in her body. That night Lindsay slept so well that she didn't hear the storm that raged outside, bringing more snow and ice to the roads.

When Lindsay woke up, the house was so quiet that she thought it must be late and everyone gone for the day. Knowing that Rebecca was planning the country club dance that evening, she assumed that she was at the club and Sidney at his law office. She went into the adjacent bathroom, washed her face, and brushed her teeth.

Putting on a robe made of white wool and covered with violets and green leaves, she walked down the double-width staircase to the receiving room that she had been in the night before; it was empty. The painting on the wall over the fireplace was magnificent with the dark cherry paneling background. The silver tea set was on the coffee table with used cups on the tray.

Touching the side of the coffee pot, Lindsay poured herself a cup of coffee and walked into the dining room. The table was set with a damask tablecloth and matching napkins in silver napkin rings. The centerpiece was a silver bowl of holly. Lindsay proceeded to the butler's pantry and then into the kitchen. The servants' table was set with a lively Christmas tablecloth and candles. Propped up against one of the candles was a note addressed to Lindsay; it was in Mark's handwriting.

It read: "Darling. Please help yourself to breakfast and anything else you want. The cook is off for the holidays and James the butler is also away. We have to rough it every year at this time. I'll be home around two o'clock and we'll have a late lunch. Love always, Mark."

Looking into the refrigerator, Lindsay found English muffins and jelly. She found the toaster on the sideboard and put the muffins in. Then she sat down at the kitchen table to read the *Toledo Blade,* the morning paper. Engrossed in the paper, Lindsay didn't hear the footsteps on the back staircase until it was too late.

A monstrous collie made a wild dash for her and knocked her off the chair. Lying on the floor with the dog's face inches away from hers, Lindsay hoped that she wasn't alone in the house until Mark got home. All of a sudden she heard someone running overhead and then down the stairs. Relieved, Lindsay just hoped that it wasn't another dog.

"Buster . . . Buster . . . Where are you?" Lindsay thanked God that it was a man's voice. Soon she saw Mark's younger brother, Jeff, standing over her.

"Lindsay, I'm so sorry that he surprised you and knocked you down."

He helped Lindsay up from the floor, and they both laughed together. Lindsay could just imagine how strange she looked to Jeff on the floor.

"Well, Jeff, I'm glad to see you. I could picture myself on the floor until Mark got home." Jeff went over to the toaster and brought the English muffins to the table. Sitting together at the table, they became fast friends and chatted for awhile. Lindsay looked at the clock over the sink and realized that she had better get dressed and ready for her lunch date with Mark. It was already twelve-thirty.

Climbing the back stairs to her room, Lindsay wondered again why Mark had to work so hard when his family had all this. The bath salts and oils were on the shelf over the tub; Rebecca was certainly a wonderful hostess. Towels were on a warming rack and the soap in the dish was imported from London. Climbing into the tub, Lindsay felt like a princess. She had Mark and was being treated so wonderfully. It was beyond her wildest dreams! All of a sudden, Lindsay heard a knock at the door; it was Rebecca asking if she needed anything. Lindsay said no and thanked her. Rebecca said through the door that she would wait in the library for Mark and her, and they would have tea.

Picking out a wool, hunter-green slacks and sweater outfit, Lindsay dressed with care. Her makeup was lightly done, and the headband of blue and green plaid controlled her curling hair. Slipping into Bass loafers, she walked down to the library, where she found Rebecca waiting with the tea service in front of her. The tray of canapes was beautifully done in Christmas colors, adding to the assortment of finger sandwiches. How was Lindsay going to eat lunch after all this?

"Tell me, dear," Rebecca began, "did you sleep well?" The smile on her face was very friendly and caring. "Mark tells me that your family is in their own business and that you have a great deal of social life in Cleveland. Mark is very much in love with you, you know." She poured the tea and then sat back on the leather love seat waiting for Lindsay to speak.

"Thank you for asking about my night's sleep. It was wonderful. Everything is so beautiful in that room." Lindsay complimented Rebecca on the lovely tea table that she had prepared. Then they sat in silence until they heard Mark at the door. He appeared, smiling and happy to see Lindsay; he leaned down to kiss her cheek. He didn't say anything to his mother for a few minutes; then he turned to her and asked how the plans for the dinner dance were coming along.

Everything was planned down to the last detail, and Rebecca was rechecking her list when Mark and Lindsay left the house to have lunch at the club. The club was decorated in a winter wonderland scene. The ceiling of the dining room was lined with sparkling fake snow.

# Chapter 6

The sound of thunder broke Lindsay's daydream of so long ago. How she wished that she could go back in time and know what she knew now. Nothing could have prepared that innocent young girl so long ago for what would happen in her marriage to Mark. How young and innocent she truly was; slowly she climbed the stairs to bed. Dawn was just breaking when Lindsay slid into bed next to Mark. Mark looked so young and innocent; she moved closer to his side. Feeling his skin so smooth and soft next to hers made Lindsay want to stay there forever.

Mark opened his eyes and slowly pulled Lindsay to him, cradling her face against his. "Honey, I couldn't live without you. You know that, don't you?" The warmth of his body next to hers only made her want him more, if that was possible. Mornings with Mark were always wonderful.

Lindsay awakened, only to find Mark gone from their bed and the sound of the shower running in the bathroom. She moved over to Mark's side of the bed and felt the warmth of his body on the sheets. At that moment, the shower was turned off and Mark came into the bedroom; he was drying his body with a towel.

"Honey, please go to the cleaners this morning and pick up my shirts. And could you bring them to the office before

12:30? I have to catch a plane around 2:30; I'm going to California."

"What? You never said that you were going out of town again this week."

"Lindsay, listen to me, and pay attention. I told you last night that I was going back to California. I know you heard me when I went into my den to work."

"Mark, I never heard you." What difference did it make if she heard him or not? He was going whether she liked it or not. Lindsay just sat there watching Mark dress for work.

"Lindsay, I don't want the third-degree look. I told you that I was sorry about last week, and this is the last time I want to talk about it." His voice was getting louder and louder, and Lindsay didn't want the children to wake up and hear them fighting. She went downstairs and made a pot of coffee. Sipping her hot coffee, Lindsay braced herself for another night of worry.

Mark came down to the kitchen and poured himself a cup of coffee, in a "to go" cup, naturally. He quickly kissed Lindsay on the forehead and walked out the door to the garage. Hearing the car pull out of the driveway, Lindsay wondered if this time Mark would remember his promises to her. Would it be out of sight, out of mind for him?

The morning was lost to thoughts of what Mark would be doing when he arrived in California, and with whom. Thunder roared in the distance, and lightning flashed in the sky. Taking her cup of coffee out to the deck, Lindsay looked up in the sky and prayed that God would keep Mark on the straight and narrow road while he was away. Large raindrops fell from the sky and pelted the deck. Wishing wouldn't make Mark faithful; only he could do that.

The rain came down with such strong intensity that the water in the creek behind the house overflowed onto the banks. The gardenia bushes on the edge of the creek bent in two from the force of the wind. Glancing at the clock in the foyer, Lindsay realized that she would have to hurry to get to the cleaners on time if she was going to arrive at the office by 12:30.

What should she wear? Usually Lindsay would just drop things off to Mark as he waited by the curb. Not today. She was to go in and leave the cleaning in Mark's office. He was in one meeting after another in preparation of a takeover in New Mexico.

Deciding that she couldn't go wrong with linen slacks and matching blouse, Lindsay hurriedly dressed. Tying a striped fabric belt around her waist, she walked downstairs, almost forgetting the receipts for the cleaning. Where did Mark say he put them? Her mind was a blank for a moment, and then she remembered where he told her. Under the desk in his den, she found the receipt. A crash of thunder marked the return of the storm as Lindsay put her raincoat on and found the matching umbrella in the back of the closet.

Going out of the driveway, Lindsay saw her neighbor, Sandy, returning from her weekly dance lesson. Sometimes when Lindsay walked by the house, she could hear her practicing her tap steps. She was so dedicated that she asked if Lindsay would come to one of her recitals and see her program. Feeling that she would hurt Sandy's feelings if she refused, she quickly accepted. Later that night, Lindsay wondered what Sandy's husband thought of his sixty-year-old wife, tapping away in front of an audience ranging from parents and grandparents to husbands and wives. Tom had been less than supportive when Sandy decided to take lessons, but he did not discourage her and only went along. Sandy once told Lindsay that Tom had abandoned a first wife and three small children to marry her. Unfortunately, they never had children, and his first family never forgave him. Sandy had tried to reach out to the now adult children, but all mail and gifts were returned unopened. At holiday time, Tom would walk the floor until late at night, saying nothing, and looking out the window, waiting.

Driving down the street, Lindsay wondered what her children would do if Mark left her. She knew in her heart and the very thought sent shivers up her spine. Mark leaving his family would be unthinkable in his children's eyes, but Lindsay feared that if it did happen, they would never forgive him. She said a silent prayer to herself that nothing like that would ever happen.

The streets had begun to flood from the overflow of the sewers and the rain-soaked ground. The rain was so severe that the windshield wipers could not keep the windows clear enough to see on-coming traffic. Thank goodness the ride to the cleaners and to the office were close to each other; traffic was at a standstill. Realizing that the traffic mess would take some time to clear up, Lindsay pulled into the Dunkin' Donuts parking lot and waited.

Lindsay still had an hour before she had to meet Mark, so she decided to go in and get a cup of coffee and wait in comfort. Sitting on a stool in the back of the restaurant, she saw Kim, Mark's secretary, come in with another woman. Neither one saw Lindsay, they were so engrossed in conversation. Kim's back was facing Lindsay, so Lindsay moved closer to hear what they were saying. Lately, Kim had been cool to her on the phone, and Lindsay wanted to know why.

"I can't wait to get on that plane and get away from the office for a few days. Mark is such a tyrant in the office, but everything is different on the road."

"I wonder how his wife feels when he's on the road. You know what they say about frigid women, and with Mark being such a stud . . . "

Laughing at their little remarks, the two women walked out of the donut shop. So everyone wonders about me when

Mark is on the road? Frigid? Lindsay wished she could walk up to their car and just let them have it, but she knew that Mark would only be hurt at work. He probably wouldn't believe Lindsay anyway.

So Mark is fun on the road. Yes, Lindsay remembered those trips, too. Dancing till dawn, room service in their suite so they wouldn't have to get dressed and leave their warm bed of love. And of course he bought her new clothes and gifts, compliments of the company credit card. The last trip he bought them twelve Waterford hock glasses.

Watching their car pull out of the parking lot, Lindsay wondered if Kim would be the one sharing Mark that night at the St. Francis Hotel in San Francisco. She pushed aside her still-full cup of coffee and motioned for the waitress to bring her the check. A sinking feeling filled her body as she walked in the rain to the car. Rain and wind destroyed the hair that Lindsay had worked so hard on, until it was a wind-blown mess.

Mark had lied to Lindsay again when he said that he was the only one going from his office. Of course, if she had called the office tomorrow and a temp answered she would have just thought that Kim had taken the day off.

Lindsay must be the laughing stock of the office. Mark had given explicit orders not to call the hotel because he would be unreachable during the day, and he would call home at night. How convenient for him to set Lindsay up so she wouldn't call his room and upset his fun and games.

Lindsay reached the cleaners just as the storm ended and the sun came out. She couldn't wait to get to the office and confront him. The very thought made her heart beat uncontrollably, and she knew that her blood pressure must be sky high.

Max, the cleaner, waited on Lindsay.

"Mrs. Summerfield. You are going to have to change the

type of lipstick you wear or pre-soak Mr. Summerfield's shirts before you bring them in. I almost didn't get these marks out this time. I told Mr. Summerfield that it was really getting to be a problem with one or two shirts stained each time he brings his shirts in."

"Max, what shirts have stains on them?"

They were the shirts he had taken to California on his last trip. Looking at the shirts and hearing that it now was a constant problem, Lindsay felt her knees buckle and give out. Memories of the past week came back. The doctor's office, the shame, and, even worse, the public knowledge of Mark's infidelity haunted Lindsay. Max caught her arm as Lindsay began to collapse in front of the counter.

"Mrs. Summerfield, are you all right? Can I get you a glass of water? Let me get you a chair." Max motioned for his assistant to pull out the bench from the sewing machines so Lindsay could sit there.

Lindsay was gasping for breath and motioned for a paper bag to breathe into; she knew she was hyperventilating. The scene in the donut shop had been the final blow to an already stressful week. What if she had a stroke? Who would take care of her children? The seconds that Lindsay was hyperventilating seemed like hours, and although the paper bag helped, Lindsay still felt weak. Sitting in the chair, breathing into a bag, she wondered if she would be able to drive to the office to confront Mark. Was it even worth talking about anymore? Nothing was going to change. Slowly, Lindsay got up and paid Max for the cleaning. Her shaking hand was barely able to hold the money. Max carried the cleaning out to the car, protesting all the way that she shouldn't drive. He wanted to call Mark, but Lindsay knew that he was too busy to come over, and she didn't want any kindness from him at the moment anyway.

Lindsay's hands on the wheel were shaking so much

that she could barely turn the car into the parking lot. Parking in the visitor's space, she looked into the mirror and was shocked at what she saw. Drained and exhausted by the morning's events, Lindsay decided to at least apply fresh make-up before going up to see Mark.

Tom, the guard, smiled a friendly hello as Lindsay signed the log and pushed the penthouse button. The office building was only six years old, but it had just been recently redone in pastels and earth colors. The elevator made soft ping noises as each floor was approached until it reached the penthouse; the doors opened into an atrium. It must be the height of achievement to work on this floor, Lindsay thought as she walked through the atrium to Mark's office. The fountain in the center of the atrium had benches surrounding it. Lindsay sat down for a moment to compose herself. She wanted to be calm; there were so many people involved whom she didn't want to hurt. If Mark lost his job, how could Lindsay put the children through college and make sure that they wouldn't be hurt by a quick remarriage for Mark? Mark would not stay single long; he liked the status that family and position gave him.

Kim walked through the door with her carry-on bag in her hand. Pencil thin and wearing a very expensive navy blue business suit, she stopped dead in her tracks.

"Lindsay, how are you? I didn't expect to see you here today." Holding the cleaning in her left hand, Lindsay picked up her purse and stood in front of her, blocking the path to the elevator.

"I'm sure that I am probably the last person you expected to see today. Off on a little trip?"

"Yes, but it's business, not fun."

"Well, Kim, I'm sure those donuts you bought this morning won't help to keep you slim for too long." Smiling,

Lindsay walked past her to Mark's office, never turning around to see her reaction.

Mark was in a meeting when Lindsay walked into his office, so she left his laundry with the receptionist. Before leaving she wrote a note to Mark to call before leaving on his trip.

Lindsay barely made it home when the phone rang; it was Mark.

"Honey, why didn't you wait? I wanted to see you before my plane took off. I wanted to kiss you good-bye and hold you one more time."

"I'm sure you did." Lindsay tried to sound as sarcastic as possible. "Max found lipstick on your shirts, and from what he told me, it is a constant recurrence that he has mentioned to you before."

There was silence on the other end of the phone, and it only confirmed his guilt. Mark was at a loss for words, or else he was in a meeting and couldn't talk.

"Well, honey, I'm sure we can discuss this later. Tim and I are just getting ready to leave for the airport. Kisses and hugs until I get back."

The phone went dead. Lindsay stood holding the phone, knowing full well that Mark was now on his way to California and they had parted with an argument. Why didn't Lindsay learn to pick her battles with Mark on the issues that she could win? Feeling depressed and angry at herself, she paced the house until she was so exhausted that she had to lie down and rest. The cords on the back of Lindsay's neck were so tight that she felt the extension of the cords swelling as she put an ice pack on the back of her neck.

Lying in bed, knowing that a migraine headache was beginning to develop, Lindsay pounded her pillows and cried bitter tears of regret. For every wonderful moment, there were hundreds of unpleasant moments to deal with, and this was one of them. Mark would be settling into his first-class seat with Tim and Kim for the long flight to San Francisco. Out of touch for hours or maybe days, Mark would be away from Lindsay's pain and humiliation.

# Chapter 7

Sleep finally came. Merciful sleep that lets the body rest and the mind escape the cruel realities of life.

Lindsay heard the mail truck long before it reached her house, stopping and starting at each mailbox. Looking at the clock on the night table, Lindsay knew that even after two hours of sleep, she was still exhausted. When would she ever feel totally rested? She pulled the satin quilt away from her face. The motion caused the quilt to fall to the floor, and she stepped on it on the way to the window. The mail truck was now at Sandy's house, having already passed Lindsay's. The sky was overcast and gloomy, matching Lindsay's mood.

Splashing cold water on her face and neck, Lindsay ran a comb through her curly hair and dabbed some lipstick and blush on a very tired face. Looking at the wrinkled linen outfit, Lindsay decided to put on jeans, a sweatshirt, and tennis shoes before going to the mailbox. The mailbox had been a lifeline for the children, as their friends were very loyal pen pals. Hopefully, there was something for each of them, and maybe a letter from Mark, Jr. for Lindsay.

It is uncanny how very quiet a house can be when the children are away. Walking into the kitchen, Lindsay put on the teapot and opened the refrigerator to see what she could make at this late hour for dinner. Everything was either frozen or looked unappetizing, so Lindsay closed the door. Just then the teapot began to whistle. She opened the cupboard and rummaged through the gourmet teas that she had bought at the coffee shop at the mall last week. Settling on Earl Grey's newest blend, Lindsay walked outside to the mailbox.

The mailman had left an assortment of bills and letters for each of the children from their friends in Hudson. Looking through the mail, Lindsay found a letter from Katie, a friend from Chicago. Katie had been a neighbor in Hudson, and her husband had recently been transferred to Chicago. Lindsay was always glad to hear from Katie; they had so much in common, including unhappy children and a wandering husband.

Lindsay looked at the American Express bill and debated about opening it; in the end she figured she had little to lose by doing so. The bill included the most recent trip to California, so it was easy to track Mark's whereabouts.

The charges at the St. Francis included a room, dry-cleaning bills, and restaurant charges. Looking further, Lindsay noticed a charge to the gift shop. Thinking back to that trip, Lindsay could not remember Mark bringing any gifts home for the children or her. She decided to call the gift shop, and pretend to be Kim, Mark's secretary.

Faking Kim's voice had been easier than Lindsay would have thought it to be. A new sales clerk answered the phone; Lindsay knew that the manager would not have given any information on the phone without identification.

"Let me just look this up and see if we still have this on the computer. I'm sure that this was a custom order, considering the amount you quoted." The clerk put Lindsay on hold, and Lindsay hoped that the next voice she heard would be the clerk's, not the manager's.

"Yes, Kim, Mr. Summerfield purchased a lovely gold

locket with an inscription. I can read the engraving if you like." Lindsay said it would be most helpful if she did. "It reads 'to BJA with love, forever,' and the date."

Lindsay's heart was racing; she scribbled the message on a Post-it pad. Who was BJA? She didn't know anyone with those initials.

The mystery woman occupied Lindsay's thoughts. BJA had caused so much pain and embarrassment for her. BJA was, to quote Mark, Lindsay's 'figment of imagination.' Mark's affair certainly seemed to be more than a one-night stand; it was an affair.

Lindsay wondered if Mark's argument with her had put him right back into the arms of this woman. Here she sat, 3,000 miles away and unable to even fight for what was rightfully hers to keep.

Another storm had come, and the curtains were getting wet from the sudden rain and wind. Sitting on the love seat, Lindsay really didn't care if the curtains were damaged from the water. She just didn't care anymore.

The children arrived home to find their mother curled up in a fetal position, not caring if she lived or died that day. Matt kept stroking her back and asking what was wrong, while Megan and Jennifer just stood there in shock.

"Mom, should we call Dad or Grandma?" Lindsay shook her head no and asked for another cover; she said she was coming down with the flu.

"Don't worry, I'll be fine in the morning. I just have to rest and drink lots of fluids. No need to call Dad; he is so far away and has an important meeting tomorrow."

Matt just looked and shook his head; he knew that even if they tried to call Mark, he would never disrupt a meeting for the flu.

"Why don't you kids go out to dinner while I rest for awhile? I'll treat you to Coco's or whatever you want."

The children reluctantly decided on Coco's and promised to bring some hot chicken soup back to Lindsay.

Lying down, waiting for the children to return, the phone rang. Lindsay picked it up on the second ring, only to hear a click on the other end. A few minutes later the phone rang again, and another click was heard. Lindsay wondered if the party had the wrong number and thought that they didn't have manners enough to apologize. If the phone rang again, Lindsay would have the answering machine pick up. The phone rang again, and the machine picked up on the fifth ring. Lindsay could hear Mark's message because it was set for two-way answering; the message left was a dial tone. Someone was waiting for a certain person to answer before leaving a message. Lindsay knew that that person was waiting on Mark.

All night long the phone rang and no matter which family member picked it up, there was a click on the other line. By midnight, the Summerfields, minus Mark, were very annoyed. Shortly after, the phone rang one more time, and Lindsay heard Mark's voice on the other end. She told him what had been happening all evening and how irritating it was. This time Lindsay didn't make the mistake of casting stones at Mark. Mark listened without making any comment and then asked about everyone's day.

"Do you think we will have any more calls tonight, Mark?" Hoping for an answer to the problem, Lindsay waited.

"Honey, don't worry. I'm sure that you won't. Have a good night. I love you."

Lindsay hung up the phone and waited for the next hang-up call. Hours went by with no more calls, and Lindsay knew that Mark had taken care of the problem. She was relieved but also knew that there was another woman in Mark's life—a woman who would stop at nothing to reach him. The next time, would she talk to Lindsay or the children? Would she show up at the door? Mark's game had taken a sinister turn, and now it seemed the whole family would be involved.

What had Mark promised that woman? Was he with her now? Lindsay paced the floor, her imagination went wild. Tomorrow, when I talk to Mark, I will tell him that I will not have this again under any circumstances or I will leave him. No matter how hard it would be, Lindsay would not have Mark's infidelity in her home. Mark knew that there was a line that no one crossed when it came to Lindsay's children and her home.

Lindsay was awake in bed, wondering what Mark had promised that woman and why she thought she could bring her whoring ways into Lindsay's home. Finally, Lindsay took an antidepressant to help her sleep and drown her thoughts.

The phone rang close to 7:00 the next morning, waking Lindsay from a deep sleep. The antidepressant had done its job.

"Good morning sleepyhead. I'm on my way home."

"Mark? What about your meeting today?"

"It was canceled, honey. Steve Miller's father-in-law died suddenly last night. I'll see you tonight. Be ready. We're going out when I get back."

"Where are we going?"

Mark told her about a get-together at Elan's that night and said he would meet her there at seven.

"Sounds great, Mark." She been dying to go to Elan's; it was the newest place at the mall, and everyone met there after work.

"About last night, Lindsay. It was nothing. You know that there is no one else for me. I've learned my lesson."

How Lindsay wanted to believe him, with every breath

in her body. She willed herself to forget all that happened the night before.

"Mark, I really want to put that away forever. You know that I love you very much, and I never want the children to be without you in their lives, or mine."

"Honey, just remember that I love you, and you only."

Lindsay hung up the phone with Mark's words echoing in her ears. Tonight would be a new start for them. She knew deep in her heart that she would never leave Mark, no matter what he did. How Lindsay wished that she loved Mark less so she could walk away.

The day was uneventful as Lindsay straightened up and then decided to look for a new outfit at Talbots. The heat was already smothering—another record-high temperature in Atlanta. Stopping at Don Shaws, Lindsay arranged for a facial and manicure appointment for later that day, and then walked back to Talbots. Lindsay was a regular shopper, and the sales clerk greeted her at the door.

"Looking for something special, or just browsing, Mrs. Summerfield?"

Putting her sunglasses into her straw bag, Lindsay said she wanted to look around a bit. Walking around the store, she noticed several other women browsing. The one perk of being a corporate wife was the money to buy what you wanted when you wanted.

Finding a simple black linen dress and matching low-heeled pumps, Lindsay left the store to keep her appointment at Don Shaws. The new shop was lovely, with the decor done in black and white. Maggie took her upstairs, where Lindsay changed into a smock. The dark cubicle was very restful as she lay down to wait for Sophie to begin her facial. Sophie arrived a few minutes later and began. Answering her questions in one or two sentences, Sophie soon stopped talking. Her wonderful fingers massaged Lindsay's face and neck and slowly relaxed the neck muscles. She felt like a new woman when she was finished with the facial.

Maggie came in to do Lindsay's manicure, and at the last minute she asked if she had time for a pedicure. Saying she had, Lindsay soaked her feet in warm soapy water. During the massaging of her calves and feet, Lindsay thought about the night before. She knew that more than a death had brought Mark home early. Mark had ended another threat to his marriage. She wondered what kind of woman would ever take Mark away from her.

Walking to her car, Lindsay thought of how privileged she was to be able to spend money as she just had. Putting the packages in the back seat, Lindsay sat at the wheel, not starting the engine, but thinking. The day of shopping and pampering did not remove the empty feeling Lindsay felt in the pit of her stomach.

Driving past Mark's office, Lindsay heard the company helicopter hovering overhead waiting to land on the helicopter pad. She wondered who was sitting in the helicopter ready to be swept up to the penthouse offices. Yes, the status was wonderful at the penthouse level, and the vultures were ready to replace the first fallen executive. Watching the people disembark from the helicopter, Lindsay hoped that Mark would never be one of those people replaced.

Stopping at the Colonel's for a box of chicken for the children's dinner that night, Lindsay wondered how Mark would be when she met him at Elan's. She only wished that she could see into the future and know where this relationship was going.

Seeing a young family stopped at the drive-thru, Lindsay thought back to when the children were babies and life was so simple. Their social life had been potluck dinners with neighbors and friends, and now it was catered dinners and fine wines from the wine cellar. Laughing to herself, Lindsay remembered the Boone's Farm wine that she and Mark had sipped under the willow tree in their first home in Cleveland. How they had scrimped and saved for that little three-bedroom colonial, and now the sky was the limit with mortgage companies. It seemed they laughed and loved better then, and Lindsay missed those days with all her heart.

"Ma'am, here's your chicken. I hope you enjoy it."

The Southerners were definitely friendlier than the Northerners, and Lindsay found herself acting the same way when she went back north to visit family and friends.

Opening the garage door, Lindsay noticed that the MGB was gone, which meant that Matt was out and about. Lindsay hoped that he was having a good time with his new friend, Phillip. Phillip was a lost child in his family group, and Lindsay's heart went out to him. He had been visiting more and more at their house, and Matt seemed happier than he had been in months.

Walking into the kitchen, Lindsay found Megan and Jennifer waiting for her at the kitchen table. The looks on their faces told Lindsay, before she asked, that something was wrong.

"Hi, what's up?" Lindsay asked as she put down the box of chicken.

"Mom, someone called today and asked if Dad was here. It was a woman, and when I said no, she asked when he would be here. I told her that I didn't know and asked her name. Mom, she wouldn't tell me her name and just hung up."

Lindsay tried not to be alarmed, her worst suspicions being realized.

"Jennifer, maybe it was a head hunter; you know how they call and are so secretive."

It was Megan's turn to tell Lindsay what happened next. "Well, guess what she did next. She pretended to be a long distance operator and called person to person. I asked for her long distance number, just like you told me and she hung upon me."

Lindsay sat down at the table, and her children looked at each other; they didn't say a word for awhile.

"Well," Lindsay said, "I'll just have to ask your father when I see him tonight." Getting up from the table, she walked up the stairs to get dressed for the evening.

Dressing with care, Lindsay planned her strategy to approach Mark. Again she thought of Scott. How she wished she had listened to him. Scott didn't come to Lindsay's wedding, although she had invited him. He sent his best friend, Dick. Walking down the aisle, Lindsay spotted Dick in an end seat on the pew, watching in earnest as Mark and Lindsay exchanged vows that beautiful July day. Lindsay knew that Scott had sent him, hoping for a last-minute change of mind. Someday, Lindsay would find Scott and apologize for hurting him so.

Elan's was jumping when Lindsay arrived a little after seven that night, and she knew she was never going to be part of the in-crowd from what she could see. The music was rock 'n' roll, and the dancers were very skilled in the bumps and grinds that went with the beat of the music. Lindsay saw Mark before he saw her; he was standing at a bar talking to a striking blonde, who kept throwing her head back and moving closer to Mark. This only infuriated Lindsay, as she crossed the dance floor to get to the bar. Standing behind Mark, Lindsay watched how smooth he really was; she marveled at the interaction. Lindsay tapped Mark on the shoulder, and when he turned his face, it lit up in a big smile.

"Honey, great, you're here. I want you to meet Becky. She works in the secretarial pool."

Becky spilled her drink as she reached out to shake Lindsay's hand.

"It is nice to meet you, Becky."

The music made it impossible to hear or talk, and Lindsay wasn't sure how anyone could think with all this going on.

"Lindsay, I made dinner reservations, so let's eat."

Saying good-bye to Becky, Lindsay and Mark walked into the dining room. They had barely sat down when the waiter approached with Mark's drink and the menus. Mark took a sip of his drink and then looked at the menu before continuing the conversation.

"Lindsay, you look so pretty. New dress?"

Lindsay nodded yes and asked how his trip had been.

"Honey, I don't want the third degree, so don't ruin a nice evening."

The subject was closed for him, but not for Lindsay. She persisted with questions that she knew would upset him, but she had to know.

"Mark, some woman called today and asked for you, and the girls answered the phone. I thought that you had taken care of that matter."

Mark slammed down the menu and looked as if he was going to make a scene. Knowing that she had better let the matter drop until they went home, Lindsay said nothing more until they were in the car.

Getting into the car, Mark and Lindsay drove home in silence, neither one of them feeling like talking. Mark went straight to bed, and Lindsay poured a glass of wine and waited up for the children to get home from the movies.

After the children came home, they talked about the movie and then went to bed. Mark was sound asleep and snoring loudly. Looking for the charge slip to see how much the bill was for the evening, Lindsay found a piece of paper with Becky's home and office numbers on it, along with a note that said she was anxiously waiting to hear from him.

Nothing was ever going to change, no matter how dangerous the affairs would be to Lindsay and Mark's marriage. The chase was very exciting to Mark, and only counseling might help. Their appointment was still far away, but Lindsay would still wait until then to confront Mark. Walking out the door and leaving Mark sleeping, Lindsay walked back downstairs and poured another glass of wine. Then she curled up in the lounge chair with an afghan for the night.

# Chapter 8

The phone call came around 1:30 A.M. the following Saturday morning.

"Mrs. Summerfield, this is the Dunwoody police. I'm sorry to awaken you at this hour, but a car registered to a Mark Summerfield was found in the Ogletree parking lot with its lights on and no driver."

Was this a dream or was this really happening? Lindsay reached for the lamp on the night table and sat upright in bed. No, this was real; the phone was in her hand, and she heard a voice calling her name.

"I'm sorry, would you please repeat what you just said about Mark."

"I really don't think there is any reason to be alarmed at the moment. Perhaps he just forgot to turn off his lights before he got into another car. As you know, we can't issue a missing persons' report until at least twenty-four hours have passed without hearing from him." His assurance left little confidence in Lindsay to withstand what was yet to come.

Lindsay told the police that she understood, and they agreed to call the other if either heard from Mark. Hanging up the phone, Lindsay quietly slipped out of bed and wandered down the hallway, checking each child's room to see if they had been awakened by the phone. Matt was sound asleep with his head buried under the pillow; Megan slept face down, her dark curly hair tumbling over her pillow like a cover. Jennifer heard Lindsay enter the room. "Mom, is that you?"

"Yes, honey, go back to sleep."

"Mom, is Dad home?"

"No, but he should be here any minute. Now go back to sleep."

"Mom, do you want to sleep with me? You know how he gets when he's been out late."

"Honey, I'm fine. If I decide to sleep here, I know that you won't mind sharing your bed with me. Even in your sleep, you make room for me." Lindsay gently kissed her on the cheek and watched the smile appear on her face as her eyes began to close. Her sweet Jennifer. If there ever was an angel, it was she.

The kitchen was as dark as the night outside. The bay window by the breakfast area looked like a sea of black water. Slowly, Lindsay pulled the Hitchcock arm chair away from the table and sat down to wait. Hasn't she always waited for Mark? Years of waiting and wondering where he was and when he would be returning.

In the quiet of the night, Lindsay's thoughts raced back to their wedding day. She couldn't wait to marry Mark. He was so handsome and charming the day of their wedding. Walking down the aisle at Saint Anne's Catholic church, seeing him approach the altar and look at her with his beautiful blue eyes made her heart race to be his wife.

Now, years later, the same look could still make Lindsay's heart race and want to be near him. No matter what he had done, there was a part of Lindsay that could not give him up. Many women would have walked for far less, but she couldn't. She remembered her grandmother telling her to marry someone who loved her more than she loved him. Lindsay laughed and said that Mark and she were so in love, it would be hard to know which one loved the other more. In her wise way, she just smiled and hugged her to her breast. Years later, Lindsay would remind her grandmother of that conversation, and they would hug without smiling.

A sudden knock at the door brought Lindsay back to reality. She jumped up from the table and hurried to the door before the children woke up. In the dark, she could see the shadow of a man facing the street. It wasn't the Dunwoody police. Who could it be? Should she call Matt or put on the outside light? She hated late night stories of people coming to the door for what was a pretense for help, only to mug or kill the occupants. Before her mind totally raced away with her, she heard him speak.

"Lindsay, open the door. It's me, Mark."

Thank God he was all right. Then anger rushed through her body, making her next words sound just like the nagging wife Mark had accused her of being.

"Mark, where have you been? Do you know that the police are looking for you?"

"Police? What for? I haven't done anything. Stop exaggerating."

"I'm not exaggerating. Call this number and find out for yourself."

She shoved the Dunwoody police number at him. As he looked at it, he put his arm around Lindsay's shoulder as if to steady himself.

"Lindsay, calm down. You can't believe what happened to me tonight. I was on my way home, when I felt sick to my stomach. I knew I had to get out of the car or vomit all over. There is so much flu going around the office."

"Mark, why did you leave the car with the lights on, and where did you go?"

"I just went into the bushes over at Ogeltrees and threw up. I must have passed out, because when I woke up, the car lights were out and the car was locked up."

"Why didn't you call?"

"It was late, and I thought I would feel better if I walked a little and got some fresh air."

"Mark, it is over three miles to our home from Ogeltrees. I don't believe you. Now tell me the real story."

"I can't believe that you don't believe me. You always look deeper than you should."

Mark turned and walked up the stairs to the bedroom, closing the door behind him. The click of the door lock told her that she was being punished for confronting him, and now she would have to sleep with Jennifer.

Tomorrow would be soon enough to continue this conversation, Lindsay thought, and she walked back down the stairs to Mark's den; there she curled up on the leather couch and watched the sun come up.

Their bedroom was over the den, and Lindsay could hear Mark's snoring through the ceiling. It always amazed her how quickly he could just drop off to sleep and put any confrontation out of his mind.

Something made Lindsay turn to the door, and there stood Matt, staring.

"Mom, do you really believe that story?"

Lindsay knew that he had heard their argument, and now he was involved in another scene between his father and his mother.

"I don't know. Maybe. It could be true. I doubt we'll ever really know for sure. Now go back to sleep, and we'll talk in the morning."

Matt turned and walked out of the den without speaking. Lindsay knew in her heart that another part of the trust he once had for his father was crumbling. Tears flowed down her cheeks with the memory of Matt's face. What could he possibly think of Mark or even her? In years to come, would she be held accountable in her children's minds for Mark's actions?

Somehow, Lindsay fell asleep, probably from sheer exhaustion of worrying over Mark. Her dreams were distorted, with Mark acting out his obsession for other women in front of her. She sat in disbelief and watched him caress and abuse the women who threw themselves at his feet. Time after time, he would bring a woman up to Lindsay as if comparing one to the other. Each time, he would return to Lindsay's side to assure her that she was still the only one he wanted.

The doorbell woke Lindsay out of her erratic sleep. The covers had wrapped around her legs and impeded her walking. She barely got to the entrance hall, when she heard Mark's voice.

"Great, you found the house all right."

In shock, Lindsay watched Mark carry in the luggage of his mother and stepfather.

"Where's Lindsay? Have you told her about your surprise?"

Mark's mother was her usual self, dressed to perfection with each hair in place.

"No, I haven't told her yet, but I'm sure she'll love it."

Mark showed them into the family room, and Lindsay sneaked up the back stairway to dress before they found her in the den. What surprise? Mark always had some new adventure up his sleeve, but usually she knew about it before his parents did.

"Mom, Grandma and Grandpa are here." Megan was in the bathroom doorway, looking as shocked as Lindsay was.

"I don't know any more than you do, honey."

Quickly, everyone got dressed and went down the stairs to find out what was going on.

Matt was in the garage showing off the MGB his father had bought for Lindsay, which, in turn, she had given to Matt as a consolation prize for being so miserable the short time they had been in Atlanta.

"There she is," Rebecca said as she sipped on a Bloody Mary for breakfast. "Mark has a surprise for you, dear."

Mark had a sheepish grin on his face, and his blue eyes twinkled.

"Lindsay, get packed. We're going to Phoenix in the morning for a week. Mom's going to stay with the children."

Phoenix? Was this the same man who had locked the bedroom door last night after waltzing in near dawn? Lindsay must have looked shocked, because everyone was staring at her in silence.

Megan walked up to her dad and took his hand in hers. She smiled at Lindsay as if nothing could make her happier than their trip to Phoenix.

Later that day while Lindsay was packing, Megan came into the room and sat down on the bed. Looking up at Lindsay, she said, "Mom, didn't I tell you that Dad only loves you and he isn't doing anything wrong?"

Lindsay nodded, unable to speak for fear of crying in front of her.

"You know that his mother is the one to blame for all his problems. She was not a wonderful mom like you are. Maybe if she had been more like you, he wouldn't get into the messes he does."

Lindsay put her arm around Megan, smelling the soap from her shower on her baby-soft skin. How could Lindsay ever take her children away from the father they loved so much? There would never be a bond as strong as Megan's and her father's.

The day passed without mention of the night before. Mark and Matt drove over to Ogletrees to pick up the car.

Mark's parents went up to take a nap, as they were all going out to dinner later that evening. The house was quiet for the first time that day, and she made herself a cup of tea and sat out on the deck to rethink the events that had occurred.

Why Phoenix? It was very hot there in July. No, something was going on. Guilty conscience or business? Well, tomorrow would soon be here, and the truth would come out.

If only Mark, Jr. could have been with the family for dinner. Then Lindsay could have overlooked her suspicions for the evening. Never would she forgive herself for agreeing to leave him in Hudson to complete his senior year. There was never a day that passed that she didn't miss him.

The family returned home from the seafood restaurant around 10:00 P.M. in time to have a nightcap and then turn into bed. Mark and Lindsay were the last to go up to bed. Walking together up the stairs, Mark pulled her to him and whispered in her ear how much he loved her.

"We'll have a second honeymoon in Phoenix. Then you'll know how much I love you."

Did Lindsay see tears in his eyes of relief that everything had come off exactly as he had planned?

# Chapter 9

The night never seemed to end as Lindsay twisted and turned all night. The house was quiet when she walked down to the kitchen to make coffee before the house guests awakened. Already she could see the effect Rebecca had on her home. Cocktail glasses and ashtrays full of cigarette butts were everywhere. Rebecca may be immaculate about herself, but her housekeeping skills left a lot to be desired.

Lindsay couldn't let this upset her, or she might say something that would cause a feud before she left with Mark. Thank God the maid would be here twice during the week they are gone. She was sure that the maid would charge extra with all the mess, but what could she do but be thankful that the house would be cleaned a few hours each day the maid came. Never did Lindsay like Rebecca, even when they first met. Rebecca was so anxious to have Mark out of her hair that she wanted Lindsay and him to go down to the courthouse the first month that she knew Mark and get married by a judge. Lindsay's parents were furious when Lindsay related the story to them; years later they still acknowledged that she was strange. Some friends and distant family suggested that there might be a little insanity in the family.

Footsteps brought Lindsay back to reality, and turning, she faced the very person she didn't want to see, Rebecca.

Her face without makeup looked as tough as leather with rivers of lines from her eyes to her chin. She had been a sun worshipper all of her life.

"Good morning, Rebecca."

Lindsay inquired about her night and asked if she had rested well. Always pleasantries between them, nothing more. Lindsay couldn't forgive her for abandoning Mark as a child and causing lifetime scares that attributed to his behavior at times.

"I'm so glad that Mark asked us to stay with the children. I really miss them."

Although she had heard it before, Lindsay knew better than to make any comment on how the children missed seeing her also. She was the typical "don't get involved" grandmother, unless it was to her benefit. What had Mark promised for her to spend an entire week with three teenagers? No doubt Lindsay would hear after the fact. Mark would not want to be put on the carpet in front of his family.

"Mark has done very well for himself, hasn't he?"

Rebecca's eyes swept across the kitchen taking in the Jennaire oven and grill, the latest appliances on the counter, and the beautiful Tiffany lamp over the breakfast table. Her mind had calculated the prices down to the penny; Lindsay knew her well. At the next meeting at her mobile home, while playing bridge, she will brag about her wonderful son and all that that he does for his wife and children. There will be an unspoken message that it isn't appreciated and what she could do to show how to thank Mark for all his long hours and hard work. Her fellow bridge players will just nod and sympathize with her. She was the darling of the park—always perfect in manners and grooming. Lindsay knew that they had never seen her the way she looked today.

"Yes, Mark works very hard. You know, if the children and I were not behind him a hundred percent with relocating and fixing up homes to make a profit, we wouldn't have all this, no matter how hard Mark worked."

Lindsay almost bit her lip, wishing she hadn't let her bait her again. She turned and left the room; Rebecca had won again.

Damn, damn. Why can't she be like Mark's sister-in-law, Peggy? She just agrees with everything Rebecca says and does. Of course, Peggy is materialistic, and Rebecca can be generous at times.

The ride to the airport was hectic because the Braves were playing a home game and the traffic was horrible. No matter how long Lindsay lived in Atlanta, she would never get used to the careless way people drove. Mark had to avoid two near misses and several road construction signs that someone had already hit and left in the middle of the road.

"Days like this, I miss the limousine service we had when we lived in Hudson."

Mark just looked over and smiled; nothing was going to ruin this trip. Lindsay wondered why.

"Honey, I'm really glad to get away from the office for a week. I need the rest."

Mark reached over to grasp Lindsay's hand, and they rode the rest of the way in silence. His college class ring intertwined with her wedding band.

Mark dropped Lindsay off at curbside check-in and went to park the car. The porter checked their baggage through to Phoenix, and Lindsay waited inside for Mark to join her. She was a people watcher by nature, so as she waited, she enjoyed seeing the people walk by. So intrigued with her people watching, she didn't hear Mark approach from behind.

"Let's wait in the Admiral's Club until our plane is called. I could use a drink after all that traffic."

Lindsay followed Mark to the paneled door with the brass plate on it and walked into a very lovely club room.

"Mr. Summerfield, welcome to the Admiral's Club. What time should we notify you of departure of your plane?"

Mark gave his ticket to the smiling blonde, and he and Lindsay sat down in the deep love seat and ordered two glasses of white wine.

"Do you mind if I check on the kids before we board?"

"No, go ahead and then I'll talk to them before you hang up."

Usually, Mark wanted to forget about family ties when he traveled, so his unexpected interest in calling home surprised and unnerved Lindsay. Maybe he was making up for Friday night; they hadn't even talked about the unsettled harsh words they had said to each other, let alone the locked bedroom door.

Of course, all was well at home. Lindsay and Mark barely had a few minutes to talk to the children, when they were paged that their plane was ready to depart. The slogan, "Delta is ready when you are," was exactly wrong this time. Boarding the plane and storing Mark's briefcase overhead was all the time they had before the seat belt sign came on and the flight attendant was there waiting to take their drink order. Mark ordered a Bloody Mary, and Lindsay stayed with the white wine. Finally, they were airborne and all was quiet. Mark seemed to be a million miles away in his thoughts, and Lindsay gazed out the window and watched the clouds go by. Is this what heaven must look like, she thought. As many years as she had flown, the same thought had always crossed her mind.

Mark must have dozed off, because Lindsay could hear Mark's heavy breathing. She motioned for the flight attendant to bring a blanket for Mark. The flight would be around three hours to Phoenix, and Lindsay hoped that Mark would sleep for awhile, as she needed to think.

Usually, Lindsay would have paid in spades for what happened on Friday night—silence from Mark for days and misery for the children as they tried to understand what they were being punished for. When their dad left in the morning, all was well, but by the next morning after an argument, tension abounded throughout the house.

Mark's sleeping face brought back memories of their honeymoon in Williamsburg, Virginia, where Mark was a six-month wonder second lieutenant assigned to Fort Eustis. The apartment Mark had rented by match light the night before he left to return to Cleveland for their wedding was a disaster.

The first night that they spent in their apartment was a night to remember for Lindsay and Mark. Long after making love and slowly falling asleep in each other's arms, the house began to tremble ever so slightly at first, only to escalate to a roar that resulted in the bed shaking violently and pictures falling off the walls. Mark and Lindsay held on to each other in shock as the roar of the train whistle deafened their screams. Mark had not realized that he had rented a house that was backed up to the train tracks. Years later they would still laugh about the apartment from hell.

Mark began to stir, and Lindsay decided to use the restroom before it was time to get ready for landing. In the bathroom mirror, Lindsay searched her face, noticing dark circles under her eyes. Two nights without sleep plus the stress of having Rebecca and her husband arriving unannounced had really taken its toll.

Returning to her seat, Lindsay found Mark wide awake and smiling. Maybe this is what they really needed, but she was still skeptical. Old habits were hard to break for Lindsay and, she knew, for Mark as well. His smile always melted her heart, and even though she knew better intellectually, she let her emotions rule her head again. She reached over and kissed Mark and snuggled close to him.

The plane landed long before Lindsay wanted to break the spell of the love and contentment she felt next to Mark. She had gotten her "Mark fix." Maybe, looking back, it was that fix that kept her so in love all these years through all the bad and good times.

The heat enveloped Lindsay as she stepped off the plane. How could anyone want to live here, let alone vacation here in July?

Mark took Lindsay's arm and said, "Wait until you see The Point, where we are staying. It is so beautiful. I can see you sitting by the pool and sipping margaritas." He winked.

The rental car was ready, and off they drove toward the mountains, where Lindsay envisioned romantic days and nights.

# Chapter 10

The ride to the hotel was beautiful. Mark, who had been there several times before, pointed out the local scene. Camelback Mountain truly looked like the side profile of a camel. The 300 SE rode as smooth and beautiful as it looked. Nothing but the best for his girl, Mark had told the Hertz rental car clerk. You would have thought they were on their honeymoon the way he acted.

The Point was styled after a Mexican villa, with beautiful tiled floors and lush plants everywhere. The check-in desk was recessed into an alcove, with stylish clothed clerks waiting anxiously to serve potential guests.

"Welcome to The Point, Mr. and Mrs. Summerfield," the clerk said as he handed Lindsay a bouquet of gardenias, lilies, and roses. The aroma was overwhelming. Lindsay graciously smiled and thanked him. Mark finished checking them in, and they proceeded to their room. The porter took them by way of the pool, as Mark had requested a pool-side room. The pool was in the shape of a seashell, with a pool-bar at one end filled with the golden people, both men and women, enjoying the water, sun, and a cocktail simultaneously. Now Lindsay knew what she had been missing all the times Mark traveled and she stayed home with the children.

The porter opened the door to their lovely suite and,

after putting the luggage in their room, left. Mark was anxious to get into the pool and cool off, as the temperature was well over a hundred degrees already. Lindsay hung up a few things before putting on the bikini that Mark had insisted she buy at Rich's before they left Atlanta. The daily walks had firmed her muscles and slimmed her legs, which, as she saw in the mirror, was worth the time and sore muscles. Mark was also looking, and before Lindsay knew it, they had put the thought of swimming out of their minds and the passion of love took over.

Lying wrapped in each other's arms, the problems in Atlanta seemed millions of miles away, and not worth the effort of thinking about.

"I love you and only you. You know that, don't you?"

Mark's lips were whispering in Lindsay's ears. She nodded yes, not wanting to break the wonderful feeling that had swept through her body and mind.

Finally, Mark jumped out of bed, dragging Lindsay with him to get dressed for their swim.

"Come on, sleepyhead, we have a whole week to make love night and day and even early morning. What more can you want of an old man of forty-five?"

They both laughed and jumped into their suits and went out the door to their poolside chairs.

The pool was pretty well deserted by the time they got there, although the bar was still open, and they ordered strawberry margaritas. Like Mark said, it was the drink of choice, and it was definitely their choice of drink. It was while they were arm in arm in the pool that Mark told Lindsay that he had to confess that the trip would include a little business. She guessed her disappointment showed on her face. With a kiss on her neck, Mark assured her that it was very little business and that she could go with him. This was a first, as Lindsay was generally kept out of his business conferences.

The pool was totally deserted by the time they left to dress for dinner. The phone message light was on when they opened the door. Mark, as always, went to the phone for the message. Thinking nothing of it, Lindsay went into the bathroom to shower and get dressed for dinner in the hotel dining room. As she turned off the water, she heard Mark hang up the phone. Peeping her head out the door, she asked who it was. Mark was lying on the bed nude and a million miles away in thought.

"Mark, who was on the phone?"

This time she definitely got his attention. "Honey, it was the front desk confirming our reservations for dinner at 8:00 P.M."

It sounded logical, but Lindsay knew from years of experience that Mark did not always tell the truth. She felt a little unnerved, but caught herself before she commented on her thoughts.

The sundress Lindsay wore that evening was a yellow and white print, and with the suntan she received earlier at the pool, she looked very summery. Mark wore his navy blazer and beige slacks and a striped shirt. The restaurant was lovely, with candles and fresh flowers on each table. The maitre d' showed them to a quiet table overlooking the pool and gardens. Mark ordered a bottle of wine and the seafood specialty of the house for the appetizer. It was delicious shrimp baked in a lemon, garlic, and bread-crumb coating.

"What do you have planned for us tomorrow, Mark?"

"I was thinking that we could go into Phoenix. and I would show you around. Sun City is where a friend of mine lives, and I thought we could stop in to say hello and then go to the mall and pick up a few things for the kids."

Lindsay agreed that it sounded fine, knowing Mark could not sit around at the hotel all week.

"Tomorrow night, I would like to ride up into the mountains and have dinner at this quaint Mexican restaurant I've been to before."

Mark looked as happy that night as Lindsay had ever seen him, and she just wanted to bask in the happiness.

During dessert, Lindsay suddenly became so sleepy that she could hardly keep her eyes opened. Mark motioned the waiter for their check, and they walked arm in arm down the steps to their suite. The sun, the drinks, and, of course the three-hour time difference had finally caught up to her.

Flopping on the bed, too tired to get undressed, Lindsay let Mark pull off her shoes and undress her. The softness of his hands caressing her skin was all she needed to pull him close and bury her face in his neck.

"Mark, I love you so much."

Lindsay was running her hand down his back at the same time her other hand was pulling his shirt out of his pants.

"We always were good in bed. I wish we could be this way at home."

Mark just nodded and continued to undress her, and she undressed him.

"You know what we haven't done in a long time?"

Lindsay shrugged her shoulders as if to ask what.

"We haven't taken a shower together, and I think the time is right, don't you?"

Pulling her up off the bed, Mark carried Lindsay into the bathroom and started the shower. Slowly they lathered each other all over, and then they made love. Never would she doubt Mark's love again after that night.

Mark and Lindsay finally fell asleep around dawn, and Lindsay knew that their trip to Sun City would be postponed for another day. She felt so content that she wanted nothing more than for time to stand still at that moment.

Lindsay awoke to hearing Mark in the bathroom humming to himself. As the water was turned off, Lindsay sat up in bed smiling from ear to ear, hoping for a repeat of last night. Mark came into the bedroom with a warm washcloth in his hand.

"Maybe this will wake up my little sleepyhead this morning."

He gently wiped Lindsay's face and kissed her hungrily.

"I better stop this or we'll never get out of this room."

Mark was laughing as he put the washcloth back into the bathroom.

"Come on, get out of bed, Lindsay. They have complimentary breakfast by the pool, and I'm famished."

Slowly, he pulled the covers from Lindsay's naked body and whistled at what he saw. She thought she had better get up before it would be lunch time. Walking into the bathroom, covered with the sheet, she was so happy. Mark had laid out clean towels, and on top of the towels was a little Limoges box with the inscription, "With all my love."

*Oh, Mark,* she thought, *you are really in love with me, aren't you?*

Mark had been standing outside the door where he could see her reaction, and when she turned, he was grinning from ear to ear.

The ride up into the mountains was beautiful. The cacti were in bloom and the colors of the rocks ranged from yellows to reds. Mark was an excellent travel companion, and they both enjoyed shopping in the little Mexican shops that were everywhere. They bought the kids T-shirts and both sets of parents china and clay dishes and mugs. Mark insisted on buying a liquid silver and turquoise necklace and earrings set for her.

That night Lindsay and Mark danced and ate tacos and burritos at the quaint restaurant Mark had mentioned. They danced and sang until the restaurant closed and then drove home through the beautiful desert and watched the sun go down in beautiful hues.

The message light was on when they returned to their room, and this time Lindsay called for the message. It was from Jennifer. Lindsay quickly dialed home and Jennifer picked up the phone immediately.

"Mom, when are you coming home?" Her voice was cracking as she spoke. "What's the matter, honey, is something wrong?"

"Mom, Grandma is so bossy. All she does is drink and smoke all day long. She said that she really didn't want to come, but Dad promised her that he would give her a free ticket to Hawaii if she stayed with us."

So that was the reward for coming. Lindsay had to control herself or she would ruin this trip. Nothing was going to jeopardize what they had rekindled the last few days.

"Mark, can you reassure Jennifer? She is feeling a little blue about us being gone so long." Lindsay knew that Mark would make her feel better, so she handed him the phone.

"Jennifer, how are you, honey? Is everything all right?"

They talked for a few minutes, then Mark asked to speak to Matt and Megan. They were tolerating everything all right but would be happy to see them.

Lindsay and Mark walked out to the pool and sat down on the chaise lounges and talked about their plans for the next day. Tomorrow, they would be flying up to Shilo, Arizona, for the day and night, as Mark had to meet with the Navajo Indians on his company business. Mark assured Lindsay that she would really love the area and the rural resort cabin they would be staying in. Mark had thought of everything, and Lindsay wondered how long he had known about this trip to have planned all these wonderful trips and activities.

# **Chapter 11**

Leaving their room at The Point, Mark and Lindsay drove to a secluded private airport, where a small Piper Cub was waiting for them. The pilot was talking to the tower as they boarded and took their seats. Mark and Lindsay took the two seats immediately behind the pilot and put their luggage in the two remaining passenger seats.

"How are you today, Mark?" The pilot was on a first-name basis with all the corporate executives from the company.

"Just great, Sam. I'd like you to meet my wife, Lindsay."

Shaking his hand, Lindsay settled back into her seat, terrified of such a small plane. The last time she had been on a small plane, she was going to a military ball in a small town at an upstate New York men's college. Landing had been difficult, as one of the two engines had caught on fire and they had to make emergency preparations for the landing. Getting off the plane, Lindsay had run to Jim's arms and cried tears of relief. Leaning over to Mark's ear, she asked him if the plane was safe. He just smiled and said yes, it was fine and she didn't have anything to worry about. Mark and Sam talked all the way to the assigned altitude level before Sam put the plane on automatic pilot and turned to speak to both of them.

Looking out the window, Lindsay saw magnificent mountains with large pines on the top of the mountains that were not covered by clouds. Turning to see the plane bouncing up and down and Sam turning and talking to Mark, Lindsay panicked and held on to Mark's belt buckle and drew Mark over so that she could whisper to him without Sam hearing.

"Mark, is our will in order?"

"Lindsay," he said, laughing, "you are a piece of work. Of course, everything is fine. Do you really think that I would take a chance on my children's welfare?"

Relaxing and waiting for the time they would land, Lindsay thought how lucky she was that Mark cared so much for his children.

Sighting the landing strip, Sam started to descend and prepare for landing. The first sight she had of Shilo was of remoteness and isolation. The airport was a one-room shack with men manually using flags and lights to guide them in on the one and only runway. They stopped about ten feet from the water's edge; she stopped holding her breath as the engine came to a stop.

The jeep that Mark had reserved waited behind the shack, all gassed up and ready for the ride into town. The air was unbelievably clear and clean. Mark got into the driver's seat and put the car in gear, and off they went. The pine trees were the darkest green she had ever seen, and the mountain tops were covered with snow.

"Lindsay, how would you like to have a summer home here?"

"Well, maybe not all the way from Atlanta."

Mark smiled and winked at her.

"Come on, Mark, tell me what you are up to."

"I will when I see how the meeting goes. Now, don't ask

me anything more and don't mention anything when we see Sally and Ned."

"Sally and Ned? Who are they?"

"Ned just joined our company, and they are going to be stationed in Phoenix. Really a lot of fun, but I think that they are into social drugs, so don't be surprised."

Lindsay didn't understand recreational drug usage among adults, considering all the news coverage of the bad side effects. As long as it wasn't in her house or affecting her children, she would not make a statement one way or another when she met them. Tonight would be dinner at a restaurant, the Christmas Tree Inn, where they would meet Sally and Ned.

The streets were muddy and filled with Navajo Indians and white men and women amongst Mexicans. Everyone seemed to be wearing cowboy hats and boots. The Indians had feathers in their hat bands, and the women carried their babies in papoose-style. Lindsay felt as if she had just stepped off a stage coach in the early years of the frontier.

"Lindsay, what do you think? I bet you never thought that you would be in such a backward area in Arizona."

Lindsay just laughed at Mark as he pretended to be an Indian and whoop and holler. Stopping at the company office in town, Mark introduced Lindsay to the staff of six who ran the office there. Beautiful Indian paintings were hanging on every wall. Jack Ryan, the office manager, came out to meet them in the waiting room. Tall and from Texas, he pulled up a chair to visit with them. On noticing their muddy shoes, he laughed and showed them his customized boots.

"If you stay around here long enough, you'll only wear these."

Mark and Jack talked a little about the boots, and then went into Jack's office for a short meeting before the meeting early the next morning with the Indian counsel about tele-phone line usage that Mark's company needed to lease from the Indians.

Walking down Main Street, Lindsay felt so out of place. The women wore drab, dark denim and boots. Here she was in a business suit in the palest pink with matching shoes that were now spotted with mud. The Main Street shops were so far behind the Atlanta stores that Lindsay wondered what she would find to take home to the children.

Browsing through an antique store, she came across a beautiful patchwork quilt in shades of amber, yellow, and navy. The scene on the quilt started with a wedding between two Indians, the birth of their children, the building of their home, and then the old age of the couple and their death. The sequence of events brought back memories of Lindsay's life with Mark. Turning to the old Indian woman behind the counter, she asked if she knew who had made the quilt.

"I really don't know. So much of our merchandise comes from estates. The young people leave here and never return, so I just buy the whole contents of a house and keep what I need and give the rest away."

Lindsay asked the price, which was very reasonable. She gladly paid, then left the store.

Walking back to the office, Lindsay saw Mark waiting by the door.

"I see you found a treasure already."

Mark looked at the quilt and loved it, saying where he thought they could hang it in the den.

Driving to their lodge, as Mark called it, Lindsay was expecting a large main building with cabins or chalets sur-rounding it. Instead, they pulled into a small cluster of log cabins without running water or telephones. Laughing, Mark turned to Lindsay and said, "Isn't it always exciting when you are with me?"

Lindsay had to agree and settled into the cabin. They both went to the common bathroom, he on the men's side and she on the women's side. Mark kept knocking on the wall to scare and tease her. She would never complain again about staying in a low-priced motel again.

Mark suggested that he and Lindsay wear jeans and sweaters for dinner, as it was a casual restaurant and the temperature dropped at night in the mountains.

The area looked very different at night, and as they rode into town, Lindsay wondered what would happen if they ran into trouble on the road. They arrived at the restaurant early. It was decorated with Christmas lights and animated elves, Mr. and Mrs. Santa Claus, and snowmen. The lights flashing on and off in the middle of July seemed so strange. Looking at the deserted main street, Lindsay wondered what the children were doing by themselves. Mark was right. It was time to give them responsibility.

Hearing a car pull up in front of the restaurant, Lindsay turned her attention to the young couple coming up the walk. She immediately liked Sally, with her casual blonde hair worn in a long shag and cut-off jeans. Ned looked like a tennis player in his white shorts and sweater. They were indeed the golden children of the new age. All of them laughed at the different kinds of china plates that their food was served on and of course the Christmas music playing continuously in the background. For dessert, they were served molded ice cream Christmas figures with hot fudge sauce.

The two couples had such a good time together that Lindsay wished they lived closer to each other so that they could visit. After dinner, sitting on the front porch with their coffee, Ned and Sally took a joint of marijuana out of a special case and enjoyed themselves. Mark gently nudged Lindsay's leg and shook his head, which meant not to say anything.

Walking to the jeep, Lindsay made arrangements to meet Sally for breakfast at the Front Porch Cafe at nine the next day. The ride home was quiet; they were both nervous about getting lost. That night, as they made love in a twig-styled bed, they heard the animals outside. Owls and coyotes in the dark were calling out to their mates.

At the break of dawn, Mark ran to the outdoor shower to get ready for the meeting. Shaking from cold and, Lindsay believed, fear of the dark, Mark jumped back into bed for a few minutes. The warmth of Lindsay's body nestled up against his made everything feel wonderful. Looking at Mark and wishing again that she could keep him always with her, Lindsay reached out to hold him tighter to her.

Lindsay decided not to tempt fate and to just sponge bathe before meeting Sally. A shower would wait until Mark came home to protect her from the animals that take cover in the shower at night.

Driving into town, Lindsay wondered if she could live in such a remote area. It was beautiful now, but Lindsay knew that winter would be difficult to withstand.

Lindsay spotted Sally first. Her head was hanging down and her long blond hair fell across her face. Walking up to meet her, Lindsay was surprised to see her wearing large, dark sunglasses on such a dreary day.

"Hi, Sally, I'm starved. It must be the mountain air."

Sally turned and looked at Lindsay. Her face was a mass of purple and blue, and her lip was split.

"Sally, what happened?"

Holding Sally in her arms, Lindsay felt her stiffen in her grasp. She had been terribly beaten; this was not just a fall. Fists had done this. Walking into the restaurant, neither of them spoke until they were sitting down.

"Lindsay, please tell Mark that I fell down last night on my way to the outside bathroom. If Ned suspects that you guessed, he'll beat me more tonight. Please, please don't tell Mark the truth, because it will get back to the company and Ned will lose his job; then it will be worse than ever."

"Sally, have you ever talked to anyone about this? You know there are agencies for just this sort of thing."

Holding Sally's hand in hers, Lindsay cried with her when she saw how brutally he had beaten her. Raising her sweater, she showed the belt marks on her back and arms. Ned was a monster. Thinking of Mark's tenderness, Lindsay thanked God that he had never hit her. Infidelity looked better than what Ned had done. Sipping hot tea and trying to eat grits with her cut lip, Lindsay tried to assure Sally that she did not have to take this abuse.

Sally's eyes welled up with tears, and she told Lindsay that in addition to Ned beating her, he was also abusing their eight-month-old daughter, both physically and sexually. Lindsay no longer could eat the food placed in front of her. Dear God, what really goes on in some homes? Never had she seen anything like this before, and she hoped that she never would again. What if this were Megan or Jennifer sitting across from a total stranger in this condition? What would Lindsay want the other person to tell her, and then she knew. Walking to the pay phone, Lindsay dialed information and asked for the abused women's shelter in Phoenix. Writing down the number and her own phone number, Lindsay walked back to the table and handed Sally the numbers.

"Sally, I know that this is difficult, but you must think of yourself and the baby. Please call for help or I will give them your name. I can't help what you put up with, but I can help your baby."

"Lindsay, please don't tell Mark or Ned, or he'll kill me next time."

"Sally, believe me, that one day might just happen, so please get help and soon."

Sally and Lindsay walked out to their cars and said good-bye. Lindsay drove back to the cabin and waited for Mark to return.

The meeting with the Indians had gone well, and Mark was in a wonderful mood when he came back late that afternoon.

"How was breakfast? Ned said that Sally took a bad fall last night so they are going home a day early. How did she look to you?"

What could Lindsay say after she had promised?

"Mark, I have never seen anyone so bruised from a fall before."

Mark stood in the doorway and just looked at Lindsay before saying, "That bad, huh? I heard that she has been falling down quite a bit lately. The baby has been falling too. Stitches all the time."

Lindsay made a mental note to call the child abuse hotline tomorrow and take her chances with the outcome. Someone had to tell the authorities about Ned.

"The funny part is that I heard that they are into S and M sex scenes in their little group. Ned had a few bruises on him today also."

"Drugs do terrible things to the mind, Mark. I'm so glad that we have never had that problem in our home."

"Lindsay, I could never harm you or the children." Taking his shirt off, he walked to the bed and patted the space next to him. "Time for a little nap before we go to the big restaurant in town with the Ryans. Jack promised a real Texas dinner and a bronco ride that will scare the pants off you. Speaking of that, come here."

Sally, Ned, and their baby haunted Lindsay's thoughts until she had to force them out of her mind. Turning to Mark, she stroked his face and kissed his lips before undressing and lying down next to him in the rickety twig bed; they both fell into a sound sleep.

The sound of sirens woke them out of a deep sleep. Turning to Mark, Lindsay asked if he had heard sirens or was she dreaming when she heard them again. The sirens were definitely in the camp park area. She walked to the window and saw an ambulance parked outside Sally and Ned's cabin.

"Mark, come here. It looks like an ambulance is at Sally and Ned's cabin. What could have happened?"

"Honey, I just hope that it isn't one of those falls for Sally."

A cold chill shook Lindsay's body, and she couldn't move a muscle, in fear that he had really hurt her this time. She hoped that he hadn't come across that number for the abused women's hotline. Mark stood next to her and held her in his arms, neither of them talking, just watching out the window. Soon a police car pulled up in front of the cabin, and a policeman went inside.

A knock at their door made both of them jump. Mark opened the door and the camp manager was standing there white as a ghost.

"Mr. Summerfield, I know that you know the Youngs from your company. There has been a terrible tragedy with Mr. and Mrs. Young, and I was wondering if you could give the officer in charge some information about them."

Mark agreed and proceeded to finish dressing while Lindsay waited with the manager.

"What happened to the Youngs?"

Knowing that a police investigation confidentiality is important, Lindsay also knew that she would be given only information that the police would allow.

"Mrs. Summerfield, I really can't say very much, but I'm

sure that Mrs. Young is going to need a very good criminal attorney."

Lindsay's heart sank to her feet as she wondered what she had done to put Sally in danger. Why had she tried to help when she should have minded her own business? Mark and the manager walked to the Youngs' cabin together. Mark and the policeman were talking outside as the coroner's car pulled up. No one had to tell Lindsay what had happened as she watched Sally, handcuffed, being led to the police car. Sally's face was covered with bandages and her arm was in a sling. Her clothes were torn and bloodied and she was barefoot. While Mark and Lindsay had been sleeping, Sally had killed Ned in a violent struggle.

Mark came back to the cabin and told Lindsay to pack. He wanted to leave the area as soon as possible. His face was ashen, and his hands shook as he told her what had happened.

It seemed that Ned had wanted to try a new technique in lovemaking that Sally felt threatened with. She refused and he started to slap her around, which usually made her do what he wanted in the past. She finally agreed, but with the excuse that she wanted to freshen up and put on a provocative outfit while he waited in the bedroom for her. Dressing with care, she put on her suggestive outfit and walked into the bedroom and did the one thing that Ned really liked to start sex with—she tied his hands to the headboard as he lay on his stomach. Instead of the whip that he liked to have used on him, she used a ten-inch butcher knife. Ned was able to free one hand to protect himself, but Sally kept stabbing him until the life was out of him; then she called the police.

Running to the bathroom, crying and vomiting at the same time, Lindsay knew that she would never come back to this place as long as she lived.

# Chapter 12

The ride to the police department to leave their phone number for Sally and the company's legal department number for the police to be in touch with was horrible; Lindsay felt numb. How could this have happened? Thinking back over the last forty-eight hours, she wondered how the couple they had dinner with at the Christmas Tree Inn could be so different from what they seemed to be. If Lindsay had never seen them again after that night, she would have never dreamed that it would end as it had.

The police department had a little jail, similar to the type that one would see in the Western movies. The sergeant on duty would not let them see Sally, but he assured them that she had called her mother and an attorney. There was nothing more that they could do. Stopping at the office, Mark and Jack Ryan talked about what the company would be able to do to help Sally. Jack Ryan promised to keep an eye on Sally and to call them with a report.

"Well, Mark, where are you going from here?"

Thinking that they would be returning to Atlanta, Lindsay was surprised to hear Mark answer, "I think as long as we are out west, I'll show Lindsay the big city of Bakersfield."

Laughing, Mark winked at Lindsay, so this was the surprise. Bakersfield, California. Mark had been there many times on business and always came home with a funny story to tell.

Feeling depressed over the turn of events, Lindsay was happy to leave this place and go anywhere. The nagging thought of when all these plans were made left an uneasy feeling inside. Saying their good-byes and driving to the plane to take them back to Phoenix, Lindsay thought how lucky she was not to be married to an abuser.

The first-class section was full, so Lindsay and Mark sat in coach. The whole plane was full, and they were lucky to get two seats together. American flight attendants were on strike, and the attendants assigned to their flight had just graduated from flight school. Not really caring about service, only rest, after the exhausting siege in Shilo, all Lindsay wanted was a blanket and pillow and sleep. She and Mark sat nestled close to each other in their own thoughts for the remainder of the flight.

The plane stopped in Los Angeles before taking off for Bakersfield. After freshening up in the restrooms, Mark and Lindsay went into the private club room of American. The soft lounge chairs and soothing music helped to refresh and revive both of them. After ordering cocktails, Mark went to the phone to call the children and let them know where they were and then called the office. Lindsay could hear him leave a message on their answering machine at home, and then he was talking to Kim, his secretary.

"Kim, Lindsay and I are still in shock over the Youngs. It was so terrible seeing them lead her away like that. I'll talk to Ed when I reach Bakersfield."

Ed was the big boss of the company and had been tying to reach Mark while they were airborne to get the details on Ned and Sally. Hearing Mark on the phone with Kim, Lindsay thought about BJA again. Who was she? Where was she? For all she knew, this could have been their meeting place when he arrived in California. Seeing Mark hang up the phone, Lindsay pushed BJA out of her mind and waited for him to tell the latest news from Atlanta.

"Ed really is in a tirade over Ned being killed. It seems that he had hand-picked Ned for the position in Phoenix and had given him a very lucrative package to come on board with the company. Now he has to do another search for his replacement, and his judgment is on the line with Don because of the stories that are coming out about their weird sexual hang-ups."

Mark sat down and held Lindsay's hand and teasingly asked if he should try new techniques or was Lindsay satisfied with their lovemaking. Laughing, she put her arms around him and whispered that she was more than pleased, she was ecstatic.

The plane to Bakersfield was a big shock. The trays and seats needed to be replaced. The pilot made jokes about Bakersfield and the type of people who live there. Sitting next to Mark, laughing at each joke, Lindsay felt like a new person. The strain of the killing had left, and now she was anxious to see this place. Landing between mountains and taxiing in on one of the two runways, she wondered who would want to live here.

The airport was larger than Shilo's but not by much. The one-room waiting, check-in, and baggage area was almost deserted except for the limousine driver with Lindsay and Mark's name on a sign. He looked so out of place that both Mark and Lindsay had a hard time composing themselves as they got into the limo.

They had a room reserved at an out-of-date Holiday Inn on Highway 99. The main road in Bakersfield was Route 99, and it seemed like every truck in the world was on that road as Lindsay and Mark tried to sleep. Getting out of bed to pull the drapes closed, Lindsay looked out at the highway. She thought she had never seen an uglier place. Crawling back into bed and smelling Mark's aftershave lotion against the bleach-smelling sheets, Lindsay wondered about Sally and what would happen to her and her baby. Maybe if Lindsay hadn't given her the courage to leave him and had not told her that something was wrong with her if she put up with all the abuse, none of this would have happened. The only positive note that she could think of was that at least the baby was safe.

In Lindsay's dreams that night, she thought again about Mark and BJA. BJA, who are you? Waking from a nightmare in a cold sweat, she reached for Mark and snuggled close to his body; feeling his warmth against her chilled body, she drifted off to sleep.

Mark pulled the drapes open, and the glare of the sun nearly blinded Lindsay.

"Wake up, sleepyhead. I'm going to take you to the best pancake restaurant in the city."

Dressing in a hurry, as Mark was already dressed and ready to eat, Lindsay quickly put on a navy and white summer jumpsuit and white sandals with a matching purse. While checking for messages at the check-in counter, they left their itinerary for the day with the clerk in case one of the children called them.

California Avenue appeared to be the main thorough-fare in town. Driving into a dirt and gravel parking lot filled with potholes, Lindsay and Mark walked into a fifties version of a diner. The noise was deafening, with the waitresses shouting their orders to the cook. The only two seats left were at a back table near the kitchen door, and they rushed to grab them before they were gone. Initials scratched into the table and ice cream parlor-styled iron chairs were the decor of the white tiled restaurant. Their waitress approached the table and pulled a stubby pencil from over her ear.

"Newcomers? Haven't seen you before. What would you like this morning? Ham and eggs, pancakes, or waffles?"

Finally she took a breath, and they had a chance to check the plastic-covered menu. Mark ordered the Hungry Man's Special for both of them, with the idea that he would finish what Lindsay couldn't eat. After she left and shouted their order to the cook, they sat back with their coffee and talked about the past days' events.

"Never blame yourself for Sally, Lindsay. You were just trying to help."

Lindsay reached for his hand and squeezed it, thinking how wonderfully supportive he was to her.

Marie, their waitress, arrived laden with dishes; Lindsay laughed out loud, thinking that they would need an army to eat all that was on the table. The pancakes were as light as a feather; Lindsay could see why the restaurant was famous for them. After paying their check, they walked out to the desert heat; Lindsay thought how much she would like to be back in the coolness of Big Canoe. Big Canoe always brought back pleasant and unpleasant memories for both of them.

Driving to the company offices, Lindsay marveled at the amount of new construction that was taking place. The new office complexes were not as stately or as architecturally beautiful as the complexes in Atlanta, but a great deal of improvement for Bakersfield. The new home areas were all walled-in in developments with stucco walls and tiled red roofs. The lots were small, and the trees very sparsely placed, but attractive to the eye. Lindsay couldn't imagine how anyone could like living like this on a postage stamp-styled lot.

"Lindsay, let's look at the model. We have plenty of time to get to the office."

Walking into the model house was very refreshing with the air conditioning cooling the house. The house was really

an entertainment house with tile and glass windows everywhere and of course the pool in the backyard surrounded
with fruit trees and beautiful bushes and shrubs.

"May I help you? My name is Monica Fairfield."

Mark introduced themselves and said that they were
just looking. They were shown through the house and into
the beautiful kitchen with hand-painted, tiled counter tops.
Mark turned to Lindsay and asked how she liked the house.

"Mark, it is lovely. I could move right in."

Smiling, Mark put his arm around her and held her
close.

"Lindsay, I'm glad you like it. I've been transferred to
Bakersfield. Welcome to your new home. I knew you would
like it when I saw it weeks ago."

Standing there in shock, Lindsay now knew why Rebecca and Sidney had come to help out and why the trip to
Shilo and now this surprise. Mark was a very cunning and
complex man, and no matter how Lindsay tried to stay
several steps in front of him, she never could. Knowing that
it was a signed and sealed deal, she also knew that this was
going to be their new home whether she wanted it to be or
not.

Driving to Mark's new office, as Lindsay now had to
think of it, she marveled at Mark's ability to keep things a
secret until he was ready to divulge them. His office complex
was totally different than his Atlanta office. This was not a
high rise world of glass and steel, but a minioffice complex
of independent offices connected to each other around an
enclosed, green outdoor garden with a beautiful water fountain. Seeing his new office, Lindsay thought how many times
this had happened before and how she was always surprised
and excited at the same time.

Wondering how very dull her life would be without
Mark, Lindsay knew that no matter where he went, she

would follow. The new problem would be disrupting the children again and she shuddered at the thought.

Loving Mark had a high price to pay, and Lindsay only hoped that this was not another startover chance for them. Mark seemed happy with the move, but was he running away from BJA or the women like her?

That night, Lindsay and Mark did not return to the Holiday Inn but to a very expensive resort called Rio Bravo. Mark explained that he had wanted to stay here originally, but it was booked when they arrived. The resort was beautiful and very lush with wonderful green trees and flowers that were so beautiful, they appeared painted. Nothing real could be that beautiful, Lindsay thought as they sat on the edge of the pool that night with margaritas and soft music playing in the background.

The room was beautifully done in shades of mauve with fine linens, antique reproductions, and quilted floral comforters. A bouquet of tropical flowers was placed on the sideboard, welcoming them to Bakersfield. Looking at the card in her hand, Lindsay wondered if Mark already had a new woman in his life in Bakersfield, or was her imagination just out of hand. Time would tell.

That night a storm came up causing the air conditioning to go out. Mark was sound asleep as Lindsay sat on the deck and watched the storm. Lightning lit up the sky and fierce thunder could be heard in the distance. Mark's hand on her shoulder startled her, and as she turned to him she knew what was on his mind.

"Lindsay, let's lie on the chaise lounge. I want you near me."

Mark lay back on the chaise lounge and gently placed Lindsay's body on top of his. Their lips meeting and passion soaring together, all her fears were gone, like the thunder, which had changed into a soft rain.

The shrillness of the ringing telephone woke them both out of a sound sleep. Picking up the phone, Lindsay heard crying on the other end.

"Mom, you have to come home right away. Jennifer is in the hospital."

Was Lindsay dreaming or was this Megan on the phone?

"Megan? I thought I was dreaming. What's wrong with Jennifer? Was she in an accident or did she fall?" Lindsay's hand tightened on the receiver, waiting to hear the news that scared her.

"Mom, she just started vomiting, and we took her to Dr. White, and he said that he thinks she has a severe case of Lupus and put her right into the hospital for tests and bed rest. You need to come right home."

Mark had picked up the extension phone in the living room and was now calming Megan down.

"Honey, we'll be on the next plane. I'll call you with our flight plans; now give me Jennifer's phone number and Dr. White's, and I'll take care of everything."

Saying their good-byes, Lindsay asked Mark where Rebecca and Sidney were.

"Lindsay, they left several days ago for Hawaii."

Looking at Mark, Lindsay again knew this trip had to have been in the making for a long time to do all that he had done.

As they packed and Mark changed their plane reservations, Lindsay wondered how she would now move a sick child in addition to two unhappy children. Mark was in total control, handling each aspect of the new crisis in their lives.

The real estate agent met them at the airport to sign the contract on the new house, while Mark called and canceled all their social engagements.

Everyone in Bakersfield who Mark worked with had known that they were moving except Lindsay. She wondered as they boarded the plane to Los Angeles what other conspiracy Mark was involved in and did it include BJA?

All the fun and excitement of the trip was gone. Lindsay thought about the latest crisis in their lives and what the changes would do to their family.

Over the sound of the motors, Lindsay kept hearing BJA, BJA, BJA . . .

# Chapter 13

Mark met Lindsay at the baggage counter, and they drove directly to St. Joseph's hospital to see Jennifer. The ride seemed to take forever even though it was after rush hour traffic. How dismal the dark of night could appear when your heart is breaking with worry.

Seeing the cross from the highway, Lindsay knew that they were near the hospital. Dr. White had received special permission for them to see Jennifer after visiting hours because of the circumstances.

The elevator seemed to take forever to reach the seventh floor, where they talked to the head nurse to get a status report on Jennifer. The nurse told them that she had been ringing on a regular basis to see if they had called or arrived. Showed into the room, Lindsay was shocked to see how pale and tired Jennifer looked in her sleep. Walking to the side of her bed, she took a step backward when she saw the butterfly rash on her face. How did this happen? They had only been gone a week and she was so sick. Had Lindsay missed something because of her involvement in Mark's escapades?

Mark and Lindsay stood on opposite sides of the bed just watching Jennifer sleep. Both of them had worried looks on their faces when the resident came in to give them an update. Jennifer was in the worst part of the illness, with arthritic pain in all her joints. By going to Lake Lanier over the past weekend and staying too long in the sun, Jennifer had her first Lupus flare-up. Jennifer had been complaining of muscle aches, but Lindsay thought that she had been too active in her sports at school.

Mark and Lindsay went down to the cafeteria and had a sandwich and cold drink, realizing that they had not eaten since lunch on the plane. The cafeteria was almost abandoned, and only the late shift was on duty. Lindsay wondered what kind of stamina it would take to work all night and sleep during the day. Mark and Lindsay were morning people and usually went to bed early. Tonight would not be one of those nights.

Walking back into Jennifer's room, Lindsay and Mark found her awake as the nurse took her vital signs. The smile on her face as she saw them was worth a million dollars.

"Mom, I'm so glad you came back. I missed you terribly."

Holding Jennifer's hand in hers, Lindsay felt the bond between them grow even stronger than it was.

"Honey, what about me? Don't you miss me when I'm not here?" Mark faked a sad face to get her response.

"Dad, of course I miss you, too, but you know that I am a mommy's girl." Reaching for his hand she held both of their hands. All was well in Jennifer's world now that Lindsay was back. Kissing her good night, Mark and Lindsay promised to be back early the next morning, and went home to sleep.

Matt and Megan met them at the door, and their parents could see how relieved they were that they had arrived home to handle this crisis. Megan followed Mark around the house, asking a million questions about their trip. Matt just sat watching the ballgame; the Falcons were on a winning streak, and very little interrupted his concentration. The mail was piled high on Mark's desk, and Lindsay just rummaged through it, not really caring what was there until she saw a letter addressed to Mark with a San Francisco postmark. This one Lindsay slipped into her deep pocket and walked upstairs to unpack. Pulling Megan aside, Lindsay motioned for her to follow her upstairs. Showing Megan the envelope, she asked that she not tell her dad that she had it until she decided whether or not to open it or put it back onto the pile of mail. She nodded that she understood. Lindsay ran the bath in the tub and slowly got in. The jets pulsating around her body relieved the stress that had knotted every muscle in her body. Hearing Mark bring up the luggage, Lindsay thought again about the letter and decided to put it back on the pile tomorrow with the new mail. She would take her chances that it was nothing to worry about, at least for now.

Everyone was asleep as Lindsay walked downstairs to call the floor nurse to see about Jennifer before going to bed. She was sound asleep and very happy that they were home, the nurse said.

Pouring a small brandy from the Waterford decanter, Lindsay sat sipping the apricot brandy and thinking how clever Mark was. Was it the excitement and uncertainty that kept her so involved with him or was it that she was not going to ever let someone else have what she wanted so badly? She wondered as she tidied up the kitchen how she would ever live without Mark in her life. Maybe if she refused one of these moves, she would find out, but she didn't want to know.

Walking through her beautiful home, Lindsay knew that it would not be difficult to sell, with all the extras that they had put in. How many homes had she fixed up and left for other people to enjoy, while she followed Mark here and there. Too many. Soon they would tell the children about Bakersfield, and there would be another round table of promises and agreements among them. This was always a family decision on the surface, but underneath, Mark was pulling all the strings, all of his puppets in his hands.

Taking down the family album, Lindsay flipped back to a happier time, when she was pregnant with their first child, Mark, Jr. Seeing them together in front of their first new car, a 1960's Volkswagen convertible, brought a smile to her face. Nine months pregnant, due any day, there was excitement even then of being with Mark. Mark wanted to take her on a bumpy road so the baby would be delivered before he left for military service. How Lindsay hated to say good-bye to him that Monday morning in October as he left to report to Fort Polk, Louisiana. The following morning, Mark, Jr. was born into a very loving, extended family of grandparents, aunts, uncles, and cousins; the only one missing was Mark. Neither the Red Cross nor the military chaplain could get him a leave. The nights in the hospital were long and lonely as Lindsay watched the new fathers lining up to see their new babies. Even though all the relatives came, it wasn't the same. She needed Mark then, and she still did years later.

The album was a history of all the births of the children and happier times. Later, there were pictures of holidays, each year bringing a new addition to the family. Mark always liked the holidays at her family's homes, as his holidays had been less than wonderful when he was a child. Rebecca, what kind of a mother were you to that precious blond, blue-eyed baby? She would never forgive her for hurting Mark and causing the scars that still showed in his behavior.

Checking the calendar before going upstairs, Lindsay realized that they only had a month until moving day. They would never be able to keep their appointment with Dr. Moorehead now. Mark knew about this move when he had agreed to see the doctor. How very clever. Mark was never showing his hand until the appropriate time to serve his best needs. She could hear the sounds of a restless sleep coming from their bedroom even before she reached the door. Looking down at Mark's sleeping face, Lindsay wondered how he kept track of everything. He never gave any indication of what he was thinking until he was ready.

Putting her face close to his, Lindsay willed him to tell her what was in that complex area known as the brain and memory. Tell me, Lindsay silently spoke to him, what is in there that I don't know about? Tell me about BJA. Come on, you trust me, Mark. For the longest time Lindsay lay like that, wishing that she had the skill to crawl inside Mark's mind and know what he knew or remembered so that she could finally be one step ahead of him.

Fatigue came over Lindsay's body as she watched Mark breathe, her eyes slowly closing and sleep taking over, letting her mind rest at last.

# Chapter 14

There was absolutely nothing that Lindsay could do about the dinner invitation they had accepted several weeks ago from friends of Pam and David Miller. Old friends from when they had lived in Silver Lake, outside of Akron, Ohio.

With Jennifer recovering in the hospital, Lindsay felt obligated to not cancel the invitation at the last minute. Mark grudgingly arrived home earlier than usual from the office.

"Lindsay, let's not make this a late night. The trip and Jennifer being sick has taken its toll on me, and I am exhausted. I know how much you don't want to disappoint Pam and David by canceling with their friends at the last minute."

Yes, Lindsay had wanted to meet new people who were raised in the midwest like they had been. Nice people with old money who did not shove all their new wealth in your face, as so many people in Atlanta had done to the children and to them. If it was truly known, Mark and Lindsay could have bought some of them several times over; they just chose to keep a low profile and be very family oriented. It sounded like Scott and Maggie Carter were similar to them, as Pam had described them in her phone call when she put the Summerfields in contact with the Carters.

Scott and Maggie lived in the older area in Dunwoody,

Dunwoody Club Forest, in a lovely, stately Georgian-styled brick home on a very wooded lot near the country club. Mark and Lindsay walked up to the door barely speaking to each other. Mark's focus was already in Bakersfield, and Atlanta was a thing of the past for him. There was no need to encourage a new friendship now that they were leaving, Mark thought, but Lindsay felt differently and wanted to be friends with the Carters for however long they were here. Mark had taken a bottle of wine from his private stock for Scott, and Lindsay had a lovely hostess gift from the Passionate Collectors boutique for Maggie.

Maggie and Scott opened the door together after Mark just barely touched the doorbell. They greeted them like old friends and seemed so pleased that they were able to come to their home. Standing in the entrance hall, Lindsay marveled at the beautiful spiral staircase that seemed to suspend from the ceiling. The staircase was open all the way up to the third floor, with beautiful hand-carved spindles and a mahogany banister that twisted and turned at each curve. The three-tiered chandelier was blazed with hundreds of lights, dimmed to just cast a glow in the entrance hall.

"Welcome to our home. Pam and David just raved about you two."

Maggie was smiling and guiding them into the living room, where another couple sat on the sofa.

"I'd like you to meet our friends from the club, Buffy and Hal."

They shook hands and then sat down in the matching wing chairs on either side of the ornate fireplace, which held a beautiful bouquet of magnolias. The aroma of lemon from the magnolias filled the room.

Scott, in his navy blue blazer with an anchor crest of red, white, and blue on the pocket came in with a tray of martinis for his guests; he just sipped from a tumbler of milk. Maggie passed the usual canapés and paté while Lindsay and Mark chatted about missing the midwest and the lovely summers there compared to the heat and humidity in Atlanta. Buffy kept spilling her drink on the sofa each time she reached for the tray of canapés, and Hal just bolted up at the spills. He said nothing but gave her a nasty look each time she spilled her drink.

Buffy leaned over to speak to Mark in the chair next to her and almost lost her breasts as the low dress left very little to conceal.

"Mark, how do you like Atlanta? Are you settled in yet?"

Turning to Lindsay, Mark answered while reaching for her hand.

"We love it, don't we, Lindsay?"

Mark was putting distance between Buffy and him, and Buffy felt it and looked rejected. What kind of a group was this? Lindsay wondered as she held Mark's hand tighter.

Hal followed Maggie into the kitchen, while Scott moved closer to Buffy, resting his leg close to hers. Pam and David would have been shocked at what was happening. This was a swinging group, and Lindsay and Mark were being invited to join their little group. Cold chills ran down Lindsay's spine as she wondered how soon they could leave without being obvious. Looking at Mark when no one else was looking, Lindsay saw Mark roll his eyes. He got the same message that she did, and for all his escapades he wasn't into group sex.

Maggie finally appeared from the kitchen, announcing that dinner was served. Scott refreshed all the drinks and filled his tumbler again with milk. Lindsay and Mark followed Maggie into the dining room like sheep to the slaughter. Lindsay only hoped that they weren't into raw sushi or strange food.

Watching Scott drink from his tumbler of milk brought

back memories of Lindsay's dad when he had an ulcer attack. He drank milk to soothe his stomach. Scott must have the same problem, Lindsay thought as she watched him drink. Maggie brought in a platter of chicken breasts, much to Lindsay's relief. After placing the platter in front of Scott, she sat at the head of the table and served the spinach salad. Buffy was given the task of serving the rice and carrots. Mark and Lindsay passed the rolls and butter; they each had an assigned dish. Each time that Buffy passed a salad to one of the men, she would lean over as far as she could to rub her breasts against their shoulder as she placed the salad in front of each of them. Maggie appeared not to notice anything and just kept dishing out the salad and handing the dishes to Buffy to pass.

Scott tried to pick up the large serving fork several times before he was able to grasp the fork and serve the chicken. Lindsay watched as he was barely able to place the chicken on each plate. The gravy boat was placed to his left, and as he placed the chicken on the plate, he tried to pour the gravy over it, only making a terrible mess on Maggie's fine linen tablecloth. Maggie neither saw nor cared about the mess that Scott was making at the head of the table.

Mark and Lindsay just looked across the table at each other, neither one of them knowing what to do or say. Scott finally managed to serve each of them, and they proceeded to eat in silence, not knowing what was going to happen next.

"Tell me, Mark, would you be interested in joining the club? We could be your sponsors."

Scott had made his move; now it was up to Mark to handle the issue. Why hadn't Lindsay seen this coming? It was so hard to be approved at Dunwoody that Lindsay was sure their connections with the Millers had been their ticket to membership.

Buffy clapped her hands like a little girl at her birthday party.

"Wouldn't it be fun for all of us to be together?"

The very thought sent shivers up Lindsay's spine. Hal just sat staring into space, not really caring one way or the other after the silent messages from their hostess and host had not been readily accepted.

"Lindsay and I will certainly think it over and get back to you in a few days."

Evidently, Mark did not want to mention the move to California. The dinner conversation slowly stopped, and they ate the rest of the meal in silence. Mark and Lindsay were the only coherent people at the table by the time dessert was served. Scott could barely hold his head up, and Buffy was spilling her coffee all over the saucer and tablecloth in front of her. What had happened to Scott; he had only been drinking milk—or was it drugs?

Walking to the living room for an after-dinner drink, Lindsay pulled Mark towards her and whispered in his ear.

"What is wrong with Scott?"

Mark just started laughing and leaned over and said, "Honey, he's drunk. He's been drinking scotch and milk all night."

So that was it. How unaware Lindsay was in worldly ways.

"Make some excuse so we can get out of here. Tell them that we have to check on Jennifer or something."

Saying their good-byes after making a flimsy excuse for leaving so soon after dinner, they walked to their car. Relieved to be on their way home, Lindsay moved closer to Mark, glad to be safe in his care.

"Lindsay, you could never be part of the swinging group. As soon as they picked up on our reluctance, their motivation for having us was over. The club invitation was only a front for the Millers and an excuse to party together."

Mark was barely in bed before he was sound asleep, and Lindsay lay looking at the ceiling, imagining the two couples together after they left. Now they would have to look for another couple to add to their swinging circle.

# Chapter 15

The night was endless as Lindsay thought about the Carters and the bizarre evening they had spent at their home. Is this the way that people meet and plan to have an affair? Do they look around and wait for the right person to add to their list of candidates for sex? Lindsay wondered what would have happened that evening if Mark had found one of the women attractive. Would he have forced her to join in their circle of sex and experimentation? The very thought made her nauseated and tremble with apprehension of what was happening in certain circles.

Lindsay must have dozed off from sheer exhaustion, for when she woke up, she found Mark's side of the bed empty. Glancing at the illuminated clock on the night table she saw that it was only 5:44 A.M. Walking into the bathroom, she found Mark kneeling over the toilet bowl, pale and shaking all over.

"Mark, what's wrong? Do you want me to get you a wet cloth or Pepto-Bismol?"

Mark just shook his head no and continued to vomit nothing but bile. Putting her hand across his forehead, Lindsay felt the clamminess and trembling throughout his body. Finally, he stood up and walked back to their bed and lay down with a cold washcloth over his face.

"Honey, I really love you. Sometimes I don't know how you put up with me and all the moves." Reaching over to hold her hand, he continued. "I come home and ask you to pick up and move the kids here and there, you never give me a hassle. What would I do without you next to me?"

Pulling Lindsay closer to him, he held her in his arms until he fell back to sleep. Lindsay moved closer to Mark and watched his sleeping face. They were so close that she could feel his breath on her face.

Silently she spoke to him. Is this how the game is played? First the eye contact and then the body language that either accepts or rejects the invitation. Is this how it is when you are on the road when you have your one-night stands? Is this how you met BJA, whoever she is?

Rolling back over to her side of the bed, Lindsay shivered with fear of what was yet to be known about Mark the man. Was Mark really worth all this trouble and worry? This was one of the days that she wondered if he was.

Feeling Mark wake from his sleep, Lindsay pretended to be asleep, as she didn't want to face him with the thoughts that had been running through her mind. She was tired of feeling guilty for having thoughts that she couldn't prove about Mark's infidelity, only inner feelings, felt in her heart. Never enough evidence to say a definite yes to suspicions of his alleged affairs.

Lindsay felt Mark's hand moving up over her hip to her breast. Angrily she fought the sheer thrill his hand had on her body. No one had ever made her feel as Mark did. His soft kisses covered her neck and ear while his hand stroked her breast, all the while moving his body closer to hers. His hardness was evident against Lindsay's leg as he moved up and down, rubbing himself and moaning with desire. Whispering in her ear, "Lindsay, I love you so much."

His lips moved to her mouth, and his tongue was separating her lips. The warmth of his tongue on her lips only enhanced her desire for him. His kisses consumed her lips as his hands began to pull her nightgown down to expose her breasts. Kissing them and stroking her hips, he moved her hand down to stroke him.

"Honey, no one can make better love than you. Would you like to try something new? I want you to get to the point that you beg me to enter you."

Mark's fingers tightened on Lindsay's hips as he moved lower with his lips until he could go no lower; in her mind she was already begging. Thunder and lightning flashed across the sky as they lost themselves in each other.

Exhausted from hours of lovemaking, Lindsay and Mark lay tangled in the satin sheets. The shrill sound of the phone broke the mood as Mark reached for it. Glancing at the clock, Lindsay suddenly realized that it was past ten o'clock.

Mark sat up in bed as if he had heard something important on the phone. He looked white as a ghost as she heard him say, "I'm so sorry. I'm so sorry. Please let me know if I can help in any way."

Moving closer to Mark, Lindsay watched him hang up the phone.

"Honey, what is it? Who was on the phone?"

"Lindsay, that was George McPherson from Washington, D.C. His son at college hanged himself last night in some kind of new fantasy sex act."

"Hanged himself? I can't believe that any sex act is that bizarre that it can kill."

Mark reached for Lindsay's hand and said, "Lindsay, there are a lot of sick people out there experimenting in some very strange ways. Evidently the person puts a rope around his neck and kicks the stool out from under himself, dangling only an inch off the floor while he masturbates. Each time the person waits longer and longer to save himself as the thrill becomes more exciting."

Lindsay sat in shock wondering how she could be so naive in the ways of sexual experience among people. Turning to Mark, she said, "Never ask me to partake in any bizarre sex act."

Mark just winked at her as she walked into the bathroom to take a shower. Mark followed her into the bathroom and grabbed her from behind as she stepped into the shower. Laughing, they made love the old-fashioned way, with gentleness and love.

She drove to the hospital later that day to pick up Jennifer; her mind was a million miles away, thinking back to their honeymoon, when she had come across a bill for car repairs dated just before their wedding day. Questioning Mark about the bill for the repairs, she heard a flimsy excuse about not knowing the roads around the base at night; he had taken a wrong turn and gone over an embankment, wrecking the front of the Ford convertible. Later that week, they had been at a party, when Rob, Mark's friend, was joking about the one-armed driver and the pretty blonde that Mark had given a ride home to several nights before their wedding. Mark laughed his way out of it as he pulled her closer to him so that everyone would see how in love they were with each other. That night, Lindsay lay next to Mark, listening to the approaching train and wondering about this man that she had married. Was it just an innocent encounter? or would it be a pattern of Mark's that she wished away that night?

Parking the car and walking to the elevator, Lindsay remembered the letter from San Francisco and wondered what she should do with it. The decision would have to be made by five o'clock, when Mark came home.

Finding Jennifer dressed and ready to go home brought a smile to Lindsay's face. Dear Jennifer, almost a clone of herself in feelings but not in looks. Megan was Lindsay's younger version. Amazingly, Mark always made a fuss over Megan, which people attributed to her looking like Lindsay. Jennifer had collected an assortment of cards, stuffed animals, and flowers from her many friends.

"Mom, look at what Tommy gave me last night."

Tommy was the latest boyfriend, and Lindsay knew that she would miss him when she left for California.

"Honey, this is an adorable bear." Picking it up, Lindsay made a fuss over it before packing the rest of Jennifer's things. The nurse came in as they were all packed and ready to go.

"Mrs. Summerfield, please be sure and follow up with the referral that the doctor gave you in Bakersfield for Jennifer." They said their good-byes and waited for the wheelchair to take Jennifer to the car.

Driving home and listening to Jennifer's endless chatter, Lindsay decided not to ruin the evening with confronting Mark about the letter. Tomorrow would be enough time to face the issue. Tomorrow, tomorrow, someday all the tomorrows would be gone and Lindsay would have to face facts about Mark.

That night they celebrated the recovery of Jennifer and the promotion of Mark with a barbecue on the deck. The neighbors stopped in to give their congratulations to Mark and welcome Jennifer home. The evening was lively with music, dancing, and conversation. Looking around the deck, Lindsay wondered who would not want to trade places with her; everything was so picture perfect. Remembering the letter upstairs, Lindsay decided to destroy it in the morning after everyone was gone for the day. Would she read it first? She didn't know, but tomorrow it would be destroyed and they would go to Bakersfield and start over again.

After everyone was asleep, Lindsay sat on the deck and

watched the stars. She wondered if the same stars were shining on BJA, wherever she was. Mark came out on the deck to see if she was all right. Sitting on the glider together, Lindsay felt at peace with the decision she made not to show Mark the letter, but whether or not she would read it, she didn't know. Tomorrow, she would know when the change of address card was given to the mailman and this chapter of their lives would be closed forever.

# Chapter 16

The movers took longer than usual to load the furniture on the van. Some of the neighbors who had missed the barbecue stopped by to wish Lindsay and Mark well in the new city.

Lindsay's neighbor, Carole, knocked at the door. Her hands were full of ham and turkey sandwiches and Cokes for everyone.

"Lindsay, how can you move so much? Every time that Mark gets a whim you back him one hundred percent. I don't understand it. When are you going to do something for yourself? I would never do that for Jim in a million years."

"Carole, I love him. What can I say? You forget that you have only Kristen, and I have four children to educate and take care of. You know that I'm not trained to support myself and the children."

"Lindsay, listen to me. Mark is going to walk some day when he finally gets bored with the program, and then what are you going to do at forty-five or fifty when it's hard to start over?"

"Carole, Mark would never leave me; he loves me."

"Lindsay, Mark loves the chase, the challenge, and himself. Remember that and you won't get hurt."

She put her arms around Lindsay; they stood and wept together before saying good-bye at the back door.

Lindsay went back in and pulled out the letter from her purse for the hundredth time, it seemed. Putting the envelope up to the window, she looked for words that could be read without opening the letter. The postmark read San Francisco with the date stamped in the postage circle. *Should I open it or not?* Standing in the dining room, she heard Mark come in the front door. Quickly, Lindsay put the envelope in her pocket while she walked to the entrance hall to meet him.

"How was your last day? Did they give you a going-away party or luncheon?" Lindsay asked.

She put her arm around his waist; they walked through the now empty house together, their footsteps echoing, as they did their last walk-through before the mover pulled away.

Mark thanked the movers for doing such a good job and gave them a small token of his appreciation. Walking to the car, Lindsay asked Mark again how much he loved her.

"Lindsay, how could you even ask such a question of me. Why are you always doubting my love for you?"

"Mark, I just worry that one day you'll walk out on all of us when you tire of us."

"Lindsay," he said as he pulled her towards him, "as God is my witness, I would never leave you or the children. What kind of man do you think I am? Remember our marriage vows before God." Of course Lindsay did, each time she doubted Mark.

Walking out of the house and to the car, Lindsay never looked back at the beautiful home that she had planned down to the last brick. The children were waiting at the Guest Quarters Hotel for them. The plane that would take them to Bakersfield left early the next morning, so it was going to be a quiet night for all of them.

The drive to the hotel was done in silence, each of them lost in their own thoughts. When they arrived, the children were in the pool, having good time. Their happiness brought joy to Lindsay's sad heart as she watched them play with one another. For their sakes, she put on her happiest face and went up to their room to change and join them. Taking the letter out of her pocket, she put it in the nearest trash container and then went back downstairs to join her family. The letter was forever silent.

That night, the children went to a going-away party for them. Mark ordered room service, and they ate dinner in their robes, totally exhausted from the move. With the strain of the letter and the memory of what Carole had said before they said their good-byes, Lindsay could hardly swallow her meal.

"Not hungry, honey? I know what you need."

Mark led Lindsay into the bedroom and pulled down the covers and propped up the pillows.

"Now don't move until tomorrow. You're exhausted, and it's a long trip from here to Bakersfield."

Turning on the television, Mark left the room and returned with a glass of wine for each of them.

The news had just come on. They showed the latest victim of the Atlanta children's murder case. The little black boy looked to be eight or nine years old; he was lying at the edge of the Chattahoochee River, where a hiker had found him. Cold chills ran through Lindsay's body. Thank God her children were safe. She prayed to God that she would never have to identify her child's body as his mother would have to at the morgue.

A suspect had been found that was tied to the murders. Watching the police lead away a young man with a full afro hairstyle, Lindsay saw his parents in the doorway. His parents looked bewildered as their only son was handcuffed and put into the police car. Feeling as if her heart would break, the mother slumped against her husband, and they wept in each other's arms.

Mark turned off the television with the remote control, and turning to Lindsay, he said, "Honey, you won't be sorry about the move, I promise." Hugging Lindsay from behind, he whispered in her ear, "Sweet dreams, I love you."

Lindsay could tell by his breathing that he was sound asleep as she lay waiting for the children to return from the party. Lindsay watched the stars through the glass patio doors and wondered how many times she had heard those very same words while lying in a hotel or resort room waiting for Mark's career to flourish in the direction he wanted. Hearing the children laughing as they walked down the corridor to the room, she smiled to herself that at least the evening had gone well for them, which should make tomorrow easier for all of them.

Megan and Jennifer were giggling over their gifts and cards, while Matt walked quietly to his side of the room. Matt was the silent one. Lindsay wondered what he was thinking. Someday all that was in his heart would come back to haunt them, Lindsay feared.

Mark, Jr. had promised to visit if Ohio State won the Rose Bowl that New Year's. Would he also harbor ill-feelings for them later, even though they were respecting his wish to stay in Ohio?

Tomorrow would be another beginning for all of them, but most of all, another thrill and challenge for Mark. The room was strangely quiet as everyone was sound asleep, except for Lindsay. Hearing the soft breathing and tossing from the other room, she walked out to the patio to take her last look at Atlanta. The wind was blowing through the crape myrtles, and the pines stood tall and straight. Bakersfield would be barren and brown after all this, and Lindsay knew that it would be a big adjustment for all of them.

Lindsay sat on the patio, watching the traffic and airplanes fly overhead. Helicopters flew low on their approach to Northside Hospital, the flight crew a smooth-working machine trying to save a life. Maybe that was what Lindsay was doing, trying to save her children's lives from pain and want by staying with Mark, or was it to save herself from pain and want? Time would tell, and Lindsay hoped that after all of this, there would be no pain or want, but Mark was a complex person, and she feared the unknown future that lay ahead for them.

The limo was waiting at the door promptly at eight-thirty to drive them to the airport. Breakfast had been a hurried meal, as everyone had overslept after the wake-up call at seven.

Jennifer and Megan hadn't bothered to pack the night before, so there was a mad dash to pack, shower, and do their hair all the while Matt was trying to get ready in the same bathroom. Nerves were frayed. Lindsay heard the bickering from their room; today was not going well. The porter knocked at the door to collect the luggage to take to the limo. Mark was all ready to go to the front desk to settle their charges, so he went ahead while she hurried the children along. All the way down to the lobby, they bickered, shoved, and teased each other. Trying not to add to their frustrations, Lindsay ignored them until the elevator door was to open.

"Listen to me. I will not have any more of this, so stop."

Sullen looks at her as they left the elevator in silence. She hoped that everyone would sleep on the plane and wake up in a better mood.

The airport was not busy for a Saturday morning, and the lines were short and speedy at the check-in counter. The limo driver had checked their luggage at curbside. Matt wandered around the gift shop, looking for a sports magazine to read on the plane while Jennifer and Megan picked out *Seventeen* and *Glamour* plus numerous candies and gums for the plane ride.

Watching the children through the window, Lindsay wondered how they felt about her. Would they remember only the negative things, or would they know that she always had their best interests at heart. Only time would tell. Hearing Mark call her name, Lindsay turned to see him motion for her to get the children and follow him to the Admiral's Club, where they would wait for the plane to LAX.

Walking through the door of the club, Lindsay could feel the strain drain from her body. The soft music, greenery, and subtle colors had a magical effect that removed all tension. Jennifer lay down on a couch and asked for a blanket. As she brought the blanket to Jennifer, Lindsay couldn't help but notice how exhausted she looked. Dark circles under her eyes made her skin appear paler than she looked in the hospital. Covering her, Lindsay bent down to kiss her forehead and noticed how dry her skin was, almost grainy. She made a mental note to call the referral physician as soon as she arrived in Bakersfield.

Megan was chewing away on her gum and reading one of the magazines while Matt was watching a baseball game on the television. Mark was reading through the relocation information that his company had prepared for him. The rental car would be waiting in Bakersfield, and the reservations were made at Rio Bravo Resort and Tennis Ranch; everything was taken care of by Mark's new secretary, Mona. Mona was to be the one who would be screening Mark's calls and appointments from now on. How many secretaries had Lindsay known during her marriage to Mark—ten, twelve, maybe even fifteen. Some were nice and some were horrid, but they all took care of Mark in the way he wanted, with utter devotion.

"Mr. Summerfield, your plane is ready for boarding.

Thank you for coming in to wait with us. Is there anything else we can do for you before you board?" Her smile never wavered as she spoke to Mark as if he was the most important person there.

"No, Susan, everything is fine and as usual, the hospitality was wonderful."

What a smooth man Mark was—a super salesman at best.

The plane was an L-1011 wide-bodied jet with first class upstairs. Deciding to fly with the children, Lindsay and Mark took two seats while the children spread out among the five middle seats. Shortly after takeoff, Jennifer was asleep and Matt and Megan were watching a movie. Mark had out the floor plans and was busily placing furniture in each room for the movers to use on delivery. Lindsay could close her eyes and reenact this moment many times over in her mind. A different city and a different floor plan, but the same.

The plane was very quiet as many of the passengers were either watching the movie or sleeping. Looking out over the clouds, Lindsay prayed that she had made the right decision about the letter and Mark.

# Chapter 17

Nothing could have prepared Lindsay for the isolation she felt as they approached Bakersfield Meadows Field. When they had flown into Bakersfield before, she had not thought about the place other than as a place to visit; now it would be home to all of them.

Glancing down on the area, Lindsay could see how barren and brown everything was in this remote place. As they approached the landing field, Matt, Megan, and Jennifer were pressed against the windows, looking at the mountains.

"How could one place be so ugly?" Matt said out loud to himself.

"I can't believe we are going to live here, Mom." Jennifer had a look of bewilderment on her face.

"Jennifer and Matt, don't give Mom and Dad such a hard time. They know what they are doing." Megan went back to her seat and picked up her magazine.

"Lindsay, don't worry, they'll adjust. Remember when they didn't want to move to Atlanta and the grief they gave us?"

Shaking her head yes, Lindsay looked out at the airport as they landed and wondered if she had made the right choice to follow Mark. The pilot's voice came over the loudspeaker and welcomed them to Bakersfield.

"Ladies and gentlemen, welcome to beautiful Bakersfield. The temperature is 111 degrees in the shade. If anyone wants to return to LAX, just stay seated."

A roar of laughter erupted through the plane from everyone except the Summerfield children. They just sat glued to their seats, deciding if they should take him up on his offer.

Deplaning was like walking into a sauna or steam room. The heat took away the very breath needed to live. The steps and railings were too hot to touch from just the few minutes they had been exposed to the sun and heat. Standing on the top step, Lindsay looked around to see the dust balls moving with the wind. The airport was a large one-room area with a small restaurant off to the side, the Skyway Lounge. The sign over the hangar advertised The Golden Empire, Kern County, Meadows Field.

Hurrying into the airport to escape the heat, they nearly ran over the locals, who were very used to the heat and walked slowly behind them. The cold air of the air-conditioning brought chills to the Summerfield family, as they now had to get accustomed to the change from hot to cold. The place was nearly empty as they looked around for the baggage area and for the rental car that was supposed to have been left for them to use. United, Delta, and American Airlines had a small stall on one side of the airport and a gift shop on the other. To get to the lounge, they had to go outside again, and no one wanted to chance the heat again, so they sat and waited for Mark to handle everything.

Mark motioned for Matt to follow him outside to help with the luggage. The girls went to the bathroom to refresh their makeup while Lindsay sat and wondered again how they would adjust to this place. Matt returned, and they all followed him into the car that they would be using until their car arrived and Mark's company car was ordered and delivered.

To the shock of everyone in the car, they saw the plane that decorated the flower garden at the entrance to the airport.

"Who would use an old plane to decorate the entrance to an airport?" Matt asked.

Lindsay thought that Matt would be in for many surprises before they left Bakersfield.

Mark pulled up at a stop light next to a car full of young Mexican men. They kept smiling at the girls all the while they were lifting their car up and down with the mechanical lifts that they liked to use for effect. Megan and Jennifer slid down in their seats and asked their dad to crash the light. Mark and Lindsay just smiled at each other and wondered what school would be like for their preppy children. The light finally changed, and the Mexican boys blew kisses as Megan and Jennifer slid lower in their seats. Matt only looked at them, called them jerks, and told them to get a life.

The sun was just beginning to set as they arrived at the Rio Bravo Resort and Tennis Ranch. The lushness of the trees and plants made this place an oasis in the center of barren Bakersfield. The mountains loomed high in the sky, which by now looked like no other sky she had seen. The pink, gray, and white streaks against the deepest blue sky looked like an oil painting over the mountains. The brilliant stars sparkled and looked close enough to touch.

The children went into the club room to order a burger and fries while Mark registered them at the front desk. Walking into the club room, Lindsay saw the first sign of interest on the children's faces as they watched the tennis game on the court in front of the plate glass window that was the wall of the club room. Jennifer and Megan had already checked out tennis lessons with the pro at the next table, and

Matt was talking about what type of tennis racket he should use.

The children were adapting a little to their new surroundings, and Lindsay watched them with relief as they told Mark about their plans for the next morning. Mark showed interest in the plans and told them to pick out a new racket with the pro the next day plus new tennis clothes. The evening was happy as Matt found the weight room and the girls were noticing the young boys at the pool. Mark and Lindsay ordered rum and Cokes and sat on the patio while they waited for their steak sandwiches and fries to arrive.

Looking at her watch, Lindsay was shocked to see that it was after nine o'clock California time and twelve midnight Atlanta time. They had been on the go since seven A.M., and now it was fourteen hours later and she was exhausted. The sandwiches arrived a few minutes later, and Lindsay ate heartily as they all talked about the new life they would have in Bakersfield.

Matt suggested a trip to the Jacuzzi before going to bed, and they all agreed that it was a good idea. The girls had already changed into their suits and hurried down to the Jacuzzi outside their room. Mark and Lindsay changed and went down to meet them. The atmosphere was very upbeat as they talked about their plans to look at schools the next afternoon. They would have to decide between Garces and West High School, and Mark would be there to help with the decision.

The night was lovely after the sun went down, and none of them wanted to leave the pool area, but everyone was suddenly sleepy, so they walked up the stairs to their suite, and within minutes of brushing their teeth the children were sound asleep.

Mark pulled out his briefcase and handed Lindsay a

map of Bakersfield, a gas credit card, and her American Express credit card.

"Lindsay, keep track of the charges so that I can submit them on my expense account."

"Mark, is there a limit to what I can spend?"

"Honey, just be careful on personal items."

Lindsay nodded. She understood that some things should be paid by their personal account and others by the company. She walked into the bathroom to wash and moisturize her face and brush her teeth. Returning to the bedroom, Lindsay found Mark sound asleep on his side of the bed. Straightening up the room before getting into bed, she checked on the children in the next room only to find Jennifer still awake.

"Honey, are you all right?" Lindsay stroked her forehead as she sat on the edge of the bed.

"Mom, I really don't feel well. Can you sleep with me tonight?"

Moving over to the other side of the bed, she made room for her mom.

"Jennifer, do you feel well enough to wait until tomorrow for me to call the doctor?"

She nodded yes, and Lindsay climbed in next to her.

"Mom, as long as we are together I feel safe."

Hugging her child to her, Lindsay knew that the bond between them would never be broken by anyone or anything.

Lying in Jennifer's bed, Lindsay thanked God for this safe trip and Mark, Jr.'s safety and well-being. Lindsay said a silent prayer that she wouldn't regret this move and that all doubts about Mark were unnecessary. Falling asleep next to Jennifer's warm body, Lindsay dreamed about Scott and how much she still missed his predictability and honesty. Someday, she would find him and tell him how sorry she was for how she treated him. Last she had heard he was a doctor in New Orleans, specializing in psychiatry, a field that she knew would only show how much he cared about people and their problems. He must have had an instinct about Mark so long ago; Lindsay should have listened to his warnings.

Lindsay woke to Mark shaking her shoulder. "Lindsay, is Jennifer all right? You'd better call the doctor this morning. I don't like the color she has in her face."

Lindsay nodded that she agreed with him. "Mark, do you think there is more going on than they told me in Atlanta?"

"Lindsay, I hope not. You know, there isn't the best medical care around here."

Lindsay got out of bed to dress and join Mark for breakfast before he left to check out the office and his messages.

"Let the children sleep in this morning and come with me?"

Lindsay eagerly wanted to spend some time with Mark alone so that they could talk about the school situation without the children present. Before she left with Mark, she walked over to ask Jennifer if she felt better.

"Jennifer, how do you feel this morning?"

Jennifer opened her eyes for a moment and then closed them. Shaking Jennifer again, Lindsay got no response.

"Mark, come here. Something is wrong with Jennifer."

Matt woke up and looked over as Mark and Lindsay shook Jennifer, trying to wake her. Mark opened her eyelids and her eyes rolled backwards.

"Call the front desk, and have them call an ambulance."

Mark picked up Jennifer and carried her into the bathroom to splash water on her face. Megan and Matt looked scared to death, while Lindsay tried to remain calm while talking to the front desk.

The ambulance arrived within five minutes to take Jennifer to the nearest hospital. Mark followed the ambulance while Lindsay rode in the back with Jennifer, calling her name over and over to no avail. Pulling into Mercy Hospital emergency room, they found a staff of medical people waiting for them. Grabbing the stretcher, they raced through the doors and into the trauma room, leaving Mark and Lindsay standing outside the door.

Why hadn't she called the doctor last night? Here they were, not knowing anyone and with a sick child.

"Don't beat yourself up, Lindsay, you didn't know that this would happen; no one did."

Lindsay pushed his arm away. All she knew was that her baby was so sick that she couldn't wake up and she blamed herself for putting Mark first again.

Hours passed as they tried to bring Jennifer around and stabilize her. Lindsay prayed as she had never prayed before, and she made herself a promise that as soon as she could, she would be out of this forsaken place. She would never again live where there wasn't a major medical facility for Jennifer.

The head neurologist walked through the door and reassured Mark and Lindsay that she would come out of the coma as soon as all the fluids were replaced in her system. Heaving a sigh of relief, Mark and Lindsay went in to see her. The shock of all the tubes and machines only upset them more. Taking Jennifer's hand in theirs, they prayed over her.

# Chapter 18

Jennifer lay in a coma for forty-eight long hours before she finally responded to the fluids and antibiotics. Waking out of the deep sleep, she looked at Mark and Lindsay and asked where she was.

"Honey, I'm so glad that you are finally awake. We were so worried that we had lost you."

Lindsay smiled down at Jennifer; she then saw tears well up in Mark's eyes.

"Daddy, I just didn't feel well. The next thing I knew, I was here in the hospital."

Hugging and kissing Jennifer, Lindsay and Mark thanked God that He had heard their prayers.

Two days later, they brought Jennifer home to the resort to rest and recuperate. Megan and Matt waited on her hand and foot, and she was thrilled with the attention. The specialist had given his thoughts on Jennifer's condition before they left the hospital.

"Jennifer is a time bomb waiting to explode. I don't know what is really wrong with her, but I can assure you that she is a very ill girl, and you must keep your eye on her for the slightest symptom."

They were in Bakersfield. How soon would Mark be able to leave this terrible place? Lindsay started to make a plan in her mind to expedite the relocation to a more medically accepted place.

A week later Jennifer was feeling better, so Lindsay and Mark began looking at schools for the children. Mark wanted them to go to Garces, a private Catholic school. Jennifer and Megan wanted to go to West High School. The end result was that Megan and Jennifer went to West and Matt was enrolled in Garces.

Tennis lessons and swimming took up the remaining summer weeks until school started. The company had a picnic at Rio Bravo, and Lindsay met some of the people from Mark's office. To say it was a cultural shock would be an understatement. Some of the men were on their second or third marriage and seemed pleased with their new conquest. Some had even exchanged partners and were one big happy family with his, hers, and their children present.

Lindsay sat under a strange-looking tree, watching as the people played baseball and volleyball. A woman about Lindsay's age walked up to her and sat down. They exchanged hellos and names as they watched the men and women play.

"Lindsay, I'm so glad to meet you. My name is Sonia, and I work for the company in the secretarial pool."

Lindsay looked at her beautiful features and wondered how she had arrived in Bakersfield, as her accent was foreign to Lindsay.

"How did you end up in Bakersfield? I can tell you are not from this country."

"I'm from Peru. I met my husband when he was in the air force in Peru. It was love at first sight, and six months later we were married in Las Vegas."

Lindsay could see from the way she looked away that she was very hurt by something.

"Is your husband here?" Lindsay could see her swallow hard as she turned to talk.

"No, when I was transferred here, he came and we picked out a house to build. He went back to Los Angeles to close up the house and finish business that he had started before the transfer. One day I walked him to the plane, and then I never saw him again. When I tried to reach him, he had changed his phone number and address and disappeared."

Lindsay could see the tears in Sonia's eyes as she mentally relived the terrible pain that she had borne from this man. Putting her arm around her shoulder, Lindsay told her that he must be very ill to have done such a horrible thing to someone as sweet and nice as she seemed to be. Seeing Mark in the distance wave for her to come to where he was, Lindsay said good-bye and told her that they should keep in touch. Walking to meet Mark, she knew that Mark would never do such a cowardly thing to them. Mark had character and a sense of family; never could he be so selfish and cruel. Later, on the drive back to the resort, Lindsay told Mark about Sonia. He was horrified that a man could do such a terrible thing to his wife.

The days and weeks blended together until it was time for the first day of school to start. The girls and Lindsay shopped for their school clothes, while Matt played tennis and jogged. He had become friendly with some of the local children, so he had a small social life to keep him busy. The resort would be sorry to see them go, as they entertained regularly at the club dining room. Tonight would be another dinner for Mark's staff, and Lindsay had planned the menu and the seating arrangements.

Meeting on the terrace for canapés and cocktails, Lindsay looked over the group and wondered how they liked Mark as a boss. Mark could be very tough and stern with his people when he wanted to get results for the company. Dessa and Bob were the first ones to arrive. Lindsay liked Dessa from the first minute they had met, at Harold's house the week before. Harold was an aging man on his third or fourth wife, Lindsay lost count when he started to talk about his ex-wives. His younger wife acted like a robot as she greeted them.

"My name is Mia, and this is my daughter, Skipper. Harold will be here shortly, as he just came back from playing golf and is in the shower."

She turned to walk away. Mark poked her on the back and said, "I'm Mark Summerfield, and this is my wife, Lindsay."

Mia merely nodded and walked away.

That night was a night to remember as Harold gave them a graphic account of his penile implant the previous month. Mia was getting tired of the erection that Harold could inflate with a small pump until he was totally satisfied. Mia had to be on bed rest for a few days because of the demand from Harold to try his new toy. Lindsay must have looked shocked, because Dessa reached over and patted her hand as if to say that they were joking, but Lindsay wondered what kind of people they were after all.

The guests were all there when Mark arrived from the office after a rushed meeting with Dan, another executive with the company. The women were still in their business suits and Lindsay felt out of place with the sarong she had bought the last time they were in the islands. Mark came up and gave her a kiss and hug and thanked her in front of everyone for the wonderful buffet she had planned for the evening.

"I couldn't do it without her." Mark beamed from ear to ear as he leaned over to kiss her again.

The nights in Bakersfield were truly beautiful; Lindsay

watched the sun set and the full moon come up. The group had finished dinner, then sat by the pool and listened to the crickets in the shrubs singing to each other. Mark was massaging Lindsay's feet as he spoke to another couple about Jennifer.

"We are worried that the medical facilities here are not equipped to handle Jennifer if her condition gets worse."

Everyone had a horror story to tell about someone they knew who didn't get the right care from a Bakersfield doctor or hospital.

Saying goodnight to everyone at the pool, Lindsay knew that she would never fit in with these people, and she felt sad, as she knew that it would be a long assignment for her. Mark and Lindsay walked back to their room and fell right to sleep without commenting on the evening.

The model home was finally empty and Lindsay and Mark went over to see the house before their furniture came out of storage. The house was to be repainted where needed and the carpet cleaned before they took possession of the house. Without the decorator's furniture and accessories, the house looked very plain. Lindsay was not surprised at the change, as she had already seen model homes empty.

"Lindsay, won't you be happy when we have our own things to use?"

Lindsay nodded yes, then looked in the drawers to see if she would have to line them. The insides had plastic inserts, so all she would have to do was to wipe the drawers out occasionally. The deck looked bare without the greenery and porch furniture, but Lindsay had her lovely wrought iron furniture to use there.

"Lindsay, let's go to the club for a sandwich and a cold drink."

"Great idea, honey, let's go."

They climbed into the car and drove out to Bakersfield

Country Club. It was beautiful, with Spanish tiles on the roof and palm trees and beautiful flowers surrounding the ornate fountain in front of the circular driveway. The heavy double doors were opened by a young man who greeted them and parked their car. Sitting in the club room, they ordered the cobb salad and iced tea. The rye rolls were out of this world, served hot and with honey butter. Excusing herself, Lindsay walked down to the ladies' club room to freshen up. The room was done in dark wood with floral printed stuffed chairs and mirrors everywhere. The maid handed Lindsay a warm towel; she tipped her a dollar. The phone was on the table by the chair. Lindsay decided to check on the children before going back upstairs. Getting no answer, she left a message where they were and what time they would be home. Walking up the stairs to meet Mark, she found him on the phone.

"Who are you talking to?" she asked.

"I was just checking for my messages on phone mail."

Phone mail? Lindsay didn't know that Mark had phone mail and what for, she wondered. They finished lunch and returned to the resort just in time to watch Matt's tennis lesson. Mark and Lindsay were so impressed by his back-hand ability, they felt that all they had paid in tennis lessons had been worthwhile after all.

The message light was on as they entered the room. Mark and Lindsay raced for the phone, but Mark reached it first.

"Lindsay, I can't believe you did that. Did you think that I had someone calling me?"

Lindsay could tell that he was really agitated and didn't want an argument in front of the children, so she walked away without answering him. Following her into the bath-room, Mark cornered her against the vanity and held her by the shoulders.

"All right, Lindsay, so you got the letter and never told me. I told her that I wasn't interested and to stop calling me, and she told me about the letter. When were you going to tell me?"

Looking into his blue eyes, Lindsay waited to compose herself before she answered him.

"I saw the letter and threw it away without opening it, because I didn't know what to do with it after I took it from the mailbox. I just couldn't upset everyone with the move so close. Now that it is out in the open, who is she?"

Holding her close to him, he answered, "She is nothing but a pest. I told her to leave me alone, but she keeps on calling. I met her at a company cocktail party, and she just attached herself to me. I know that it is hard to believe, but do you think I'd give up everything for that psycho?"

"Mark, I don't know what to believe anymore."

Walking away, Lindsay went down to the patio and watched the sunset. She really didn't want to know anymore about the letter or the person who wrote it. BJA had finally surfaced, and now Lindsay would have to deal with that. And confronting Mark, would she be next or the children?

Lindsay saw Mark walking over to the tennis courts to meet the children for dinner. The wind had picked up, and the trees bent over and swayed in the breeze. The sudden pending storm was like her marriage, thought Lindsay. One minute it was smooth, and the next minute it was stormy. When would the smooth times outweigh the storms, Lindsay wondered as she walked over to the clubhouse to meet her family.

# Chapter 19

The first day of school was a disaster. After Mark dropped the children off at school, Lindsay went over to the new house to wait for the movers to arrive. Walking through the empty house with her coffee and sausage biscuit from McDonald's, she mentally placed the furniture where it should be. Mark had left his floor plans on the kitchen counter for the movers to follow.

The phone rang just as the movers pulled up to the front door with the furniture. "Hello?" Lindsay said as she was letting the movers in to look over the house.

"Mom, come get me."

It was Jennifer.

"Honey, what's wrong?" Lindsay could hear her crying on the phone as she waited for an answer.

"Just come get me. I'll be waiting outside." Jennifer hung up before Lindsay found out any more information. Lindsay told the movers to start unloading while she picked up Jennifer.

Driving up to West High, Lindsay saw the police cars and the ambulance before she saw Jennifer standing away from the scene. Seeing Lindsay, Jennifer ran to the car. As she approached the car, Lindsay could see how pale she was and the tears that were rolling down her face.

"Honey, what happened?"

Before she could answer, she started to vomit all over the front seat of the car. Grabbing the Kleenex from the back seat, Lindsay held the Kleenex over her mouth.

Pulling away from the school, Lindsay held Jennifer's head on her leg and stroked her face. She would have to wait until later to see what had upset her so. The movers were already at work when they arrived back at the house.

The way to the upstairs bathroom was blocked, so they went to the hall powder room to clean up. Sitting down on the toilet seat, Lindsay sponged Jennifer's face with a cool cloth. Finally, the color returned to her face and she appeared calm. Opening the box marked linens, Lindsay pulled a pillow and blanket out of the box and made a make-shift bed for her in the master bedroom. Questions would have to wait until later, as Lindsay wanted her to rest and feel like talking before she asked about what had happened at school.

Lindsay called Mark at the office and relayed what had happened to Jennifer. He said to let her rest, and he would call the principal to find out what had happened. Mark took charge of the situation, while Lindsay went back to instruct the movers on the furniture.

A knock at the door broke Lindsay's concentration. As she opened the door, there was a bouquet of flowers for her. Opening up the card, Lindsay realized that it was from Mark. It read, "Thank you for always being behind me, Love, Mark."

"Who are the flowers from?" It was Jennifer standing behind her.

"They are from Dad." The bouquet was a beautiful fall arrangement of mixed flowers. "Do you want to talk now?"

"Mom, can we go back to Hudson? I am so scared to be out here with the Mexicans and blacks fighting all the time.

They sit across from each other and egg each other on until they get into a fight."

Lindsay waited to hear what had happened, but she was afraid to ask Jennifer and have her get upset.

"Mom, do you know why I left school this morning? A boy touched another boy's bike, and he slit his leg with a knife, and this boy was standing next to me. The blood was everywhere, and he was crying. This morning we had a knife check to see if the knives that kids carry are a legal size to be carried to school."

Lindsay sat down next to her on the steps and rocked her in her arms and wondered if they would survive this place.

Mark arrived with pizza and Cokes for the movers and them. Lindsay thanked him for the flowers, and they kissed.

"Honey, if I told you once, I've told you a hundred times, I wouldn't be where I am if it wasn't for you."

Feeling a sudden warmth come over her body, Lindsay knew that Mark would always remember what she had done to support him in his career. They sat on their patio, the three of them, and talked about their day.

"Jennifer, I talked to Mr. Wilson, the principal, about what happened today. He assured me that he is taking precautions to safeguard the students and not to worry."

Lindsay could see Jennifer swallow hard as she recalled the incident. Mark left to go back to the office, and Jennifer took a portable television upstairs to watch her soap operas and write letters to her friends in Hudson and Atlanta.

The phone rang. It was Megan wondering where Jennifer was. Lindsay explained what had happened and asked if she wanted her to pick her up.

"No, Mom, I'll walk with a girl that lives on our street. She seems real nice, and we are going to the mall this Saturday together."

Hanging up the phone, Lindsay felt relieved that Megan had made a friend. Now she would have to wait for Matt to see how his day had gone. An hour later, Lindsay heard the MGB pull into the garage; Matt was home.

"Mom, where are you?"

Lindsay could tell that he was in a good mood from his voice. "Hi, honey, I'm upstairs. How was school?"

"Great, I made the football team as a wide receiver, and we have a practice game next Friday in Fresno."

Two out of three kids happy today was a real uplift for Lindsay. Mark would be happy to hear that everything was going well for Matt and Megan. Looking at the clock, Lindsay realized that Mark, Jr. had completed his first day of college at Ohio State. As soon as Mark arrived home, they would all call the oldest son and see how his day went.

The evening was one of fun and laughter as they talked to Mark, Jr. at OSU before everyone went to Oshman's to buy football shoes and practice pants and sweatshirts for Matt. The girls and Lindsay spent time in the ladies' area, looking at jogging suits. They stopped at Mexicali's and ate tacos and chips and salsa. Driving back to the resort to finish packing for the final move to their house, Lindsay felt happy for the first time since they arrived in Bakersfield.

The drive to Fresno was long and lonely in the desert area. Mark appeared preoccupied and distant.

"Mark, is something bothering you?"

Turning to look at Lindsay, he snapped, "Why does something have to be always bothering me if I'm not smiling or happy about everything?"

Lindsay decided to leave him alone for the rest of the drive. They pulled into Fresno High School. Lindsay wondered about the game that night. The people looked rough and blue-collared as they walked into the stadium. She hoped that it would not be a rough game and no one would get hurt, especially Matt.

Sitting in the bleachers, Lindsay watched Garces warm up. They looked like shrimps compared to the other team. Mark and Lindsay walked down to the track to watch the boys warm up, and as they approached the team, a large, burly man walked up to them and raised a truckers' flash light over his head as if to hit them.

"You better get out of here or I'll call the police. We don't like strangers by the team."

"Strangers? I'm a parent, and I don't like your attitude."

Mark was furious as he and Lindsay stood facing the man. The coach came up and apologized, but security was tight at all football games. Players and cheerleaders were regularly beaten up by the losing team.

Walking back to the bleachers, Mark and Lindsay sat down in silence. An announcement came over the loud-speaker to get refreshments before the bleachers were locked at the start of the game.

"Mark, where are we? I never had to be locked up at a game before."

"Welcome to Bakersfield, Lindsay."

She and Mark watched the game with mixed feelings. If Garces won, would the other team beat them up? And if they lost, how would they feel?

"Lindsay, Matt is going to drive home with us for protection tonight. I don't want to have to worry about his safety."

Lindsay nodded in agreement and waited for the longest game in her memory to be over. Thinking back to Hudson High School and Dunwoody High School football games, she realized even more that she had to get out of there soon and feel safe again.

All through the game, Mark and Lindsay prayed that

whatever the outcome of the game, they would all get home safely. The half-time entertainment was a mixture of cheers and boos. When the home team band played, the cheers rumbled through the stadium and the boos deafened the music as Garces's band played. Lindsay nearly ran to the car as Mark pushed Matt behind her to escape the crowd, which was very angry over the upset of Garces's winning, as they had been considered an underdog.

The ride home was in silence as they were all lost in their own thoughts. The joy of Matt's touchdown was not even mentioned as Mark sped toward the Bakersfield city limits.

# Chapter 20

"Mom, Dad said that he wouldn't be traveling as much if we moved here." Matt was really upset about the father-son breakfast that Mark would have to miss as a result of a last-minute business trip to Boston.

"Matt, come on and give him a break. Since we came here, he has really tried to be home almost every night and do things with all of us."

Matt just walked out of the room, mumbling to himself that they should all wait, because it wasn't going to last and Dad would be on the road again.

The next week would be Matt's eighteenth birthday, and Lindsay wondered how they should celebrate the big year for him. Her parents were unable to fly out, and she knew few of his friends could. Maybe it would have to be just a family affair. Matt had seen a velour shirt that was for sale at the Bakersfield Country Club pro-shop; Lindsay mentally put it on her list to buy for him.

Mark arrived late that night from work. Walking into the family room from the garage, she knew instantly that this was not going to be a good night to bring up anything unpleasant to Mark. His sullen face made her wonder what had happened at the office that day. She weighed each word she spoke to him as he undressed in their bedroom.

"Wasn't it a beautiful fall day today? I bought a few shrubs at the K-Mart floral shop, where I met a lady who sold me one of her own olive trees from her yard. She was so funny, telling me that her olive trees were better and more reasonable."

Mark just kept hanging up his clothes and not commenting. Walking to the kitchen to warm up his dinner, Lindsay thought that something was really bothering Mark. But what? She served his dinner on a TV tray in the family room while they watched "St. Elsewhere" on the tube. Usually Mark made a comment or two about his favorite program, but tonight he barely watched. He seemed easily distracted as they barely watched the news before going to their room for the night. Lying next to Mark and listening to his snoring, Lindsay knew that they were in for another catastrophe and that this one would be difficult to fix. The sprinkler system came on at four o'clock. Lindsay was still awake, with Matt's lingering words in her mind. "Just wait," he had said, and now she would have to wait it out to see what was going on in that mysterious mind of Mark's.

The rest of the week passed in a blur, with Mark staying late at the office and Matt's football practices. The girls were adjusting to the social and cultural differences at school, and the fights were under control between the Mexicans and blacks.

"Honey, let's go out for dinner alone tonight." Mark was dressing for work and appeared in a good mood for once.

"Sounds great. Where do you want to go?"

Putting his suit jacket on, he turned and said, "Let's fly down to LA on the company plane and eat at one of my favorite places."

Lindsay couldn't imagine flying somewhere for dinner, but the very thought excited her. "I can't wait. What time and how dressy is the restaurant?"

Smiling, Mark handed her an envelope with five hundred dollars in it and said, "Buy yourself something sexy and expensive and all the accessories that go with it. Also, tell the kids that we'll be spending the night and not returning until tomorrow afternoon, late."

Lindsay was speechless as she watched him lean over to kiss her good-bye.

Looking at the envelope, Lindsay wondered where she would find anything high fashioned in Bakersfield. She called her friend Dessa and asked where a really great place to shop was. Dessa said to go to Mr. C's for a truly wonderful makeover and next door to Mrs. C's for a great dress. Looking up their address, Lindsay made an appointment for a wash, set, and facial after she shopped next door.

Well, Lindsay had to admit that it wasn't the quality of the stores in Atlanta, but it would do until she had a chance to shop in L.A. The dress the salesgirl brought out was a Jessica McClintock emerald green sheath with lace inserts. The shoes she bought and the bag were in the same colors. Going next door, she allowed them to massage her neck and face. Walking out of the shop with her package, she looked at her watch; it was only another hour before Mark would be home to pack for their trip. The garage door was open as she approached the driveway, and she could see Mark sitting in his car, talking on his mobile phone. Lindsay parked the car on the street and walked up to his car without him seeing her.

"I told you before to leave me alone. When are you going to listen?"

The other person on the phone was talking back to him, and Lindsay could see his facial twitches. He always twitched when he was agitated.

"I'm telling you again to stop calling me at work, or else I'll call an attorney and sue you for harassment." Mark pounded the dashboard and said, "I was as willing as you were, so don't try to blackmail me to my wife." With that he hung up the phone and opened the door to see Lindsay standing there.

The look on her face told him that she had heard the conversation.

"Lindsay, let me explain." Dropping the packages on the garage floor, Lindsay walked into the house and into their room, where she locked the door.

"Please let me explain. I don't want to ruin everything we have together."

Lindsay sobbed into the pillows.

They didn't go to LA on the private jet or anywhere else that weekend, as Lindsay barely spoke to Mark. Before the children came home, Lindsay made up a story to tell them, that the jet had mechanical troubles and they would go another time. Mark stopped begging behind the door and went back to the office to work, or if the truth be known, to call his friend and tell her that Lindsay knew about her.

Washing her face, Lindsay met the children at the door and pretended that she was disappointed over the turn of events. The girls were so sympathetic as they looked at her dress and new hair style. Matt didn't say anything, but Lindsay knew that he knew that she wasn't telling the truth. Mark slept in their bed that night only because she didn't know where to put him without the children knowing that she had lied to them. She carefully remade the bed and put two sheets on the top so that they would not be bodily touching each other. She heard the sprinklers come on again at dawn.

The next morning, Lindsay called New Orleans information and asked for Dr. Scott Stewart. The operator asked if she wanted his office or home number.

"Please give me his office number." Lindsay didn't want

to bother him at home, or maybe it was that she didn't want to hear the voice of the person who took her place in Scott's heart. After writing down the number, she looked at the clock and knew that he would probably be at the office, as it was a little after 10:00 A.M. in New Orleans. She put the number down and went to pour herself a cup of coffee and think about what she would say to Scott if he took her call and how she would feel if he didn't. Realizing that she couldn't be hurt any more than she had already been by Mark, Lindsay picked up the phone and dialed Scott's number.

Lindsay's hand was shaking as she dialed his number. How long had it been? Over twenty years, and now she was going to tell him what she always knew in her heart, that she had made a terrible mistake in letting him out of her life. The love she had for Mark was different from the love that she had for Scott; Scott's love was free of strings and hurts while Mark's love had a high price to pay.

The phone ring startled Lindsay, and she felt as if her heart was beating uncontrollably. Was she crazy? The ringing stopped and a woman's voice announced, "Doctor's office."

"May I speak to Dr. Stewart, please."

"Who's calling?"

The pounding of Lindsay's heart was deafening as she answered, "Lindsay Summerfield, an old friend."

The phone was put on hold, and Lindsay waited for her to come back with a message from Scott. Seconds felt like hours as she waited listening to music on the hold line. What was that song again? Oh yes, it was "Spanish Eyes," one of the songs from her dance class at Gilmour Academy. Remembering her white gloves and first pair of high-heeled shoes and her partner, Lindsay smiled to herself. She had come a long way since then and wanted nothing more than to be that innocent again.

"Lindsay, is this you? I can't believe it."

It was Scott, dear Scott, sounding just like he did over twenty years ago.

"Scott, yes, it's me. I've been thinking about you lately, and I thought I would call and see how you are."

Relaxed, Lindsay sat down in the captain's chair and picked up her cup of coffee.

"Well, you have really made my day, as I have been thinking about you also."

They talked about his wife and children, and Lindsay told him what Mark was doing and the ages and sexes of her children.

"Lindsay, I'm sorry that we parted like we did, but I felt strongly about your life with Mark. I guess I really read Mark wrong, as it sounds like everything is fine with you two."

What could Lindsay say? If she told him the truth, he would wonder about the dependency she had for Mark. The best thing would be to say nothing at this time.

"Scott, I called to tell you that I am very sorry about the way I treated you, and I want to apologize and, hopefully, we will see each other again soon."

Telling Lindsay that there was no need to apologize, they talked about mutual friends and trivial things before it was time to hang up.

"Scott, take care of yourself and keep in touch."

Lindsay gave him her phone number, and he gave her his home number in case she got to New Orleans. She didn't want the call to end, but she could hear him giving instructions to his nurse while they talked.

"Lindsay, remember that I care about you, and if you ever want to talk to me, call me. To tell you the truth, I never really got over you, and I still am in some ways in love with you, always have been, I guess. Remember that and keep in touch."

Saying good-bye, tears ran down Lindsay's face as she thought about Mark and the cost of his love both mentally and emotionally.

# Chapter 21

Scott's phone call stayed in Lindsay's mind as she dutifully went through the week performing all her tasks as a wife and mother. Mark and Lindsay were civil in front of the children, but in private they barely talked. The phone call on the mobile phone was never mentioned again, although Mark wanted to cleanse his soul and admit his involvement, but she didn't want to be father confessor again for him. Let him suffer in silence or go to confession.

The phone rang just as Lindsay was coming in the door from grocery shopping. "Mrs. Summerfield, you don't know me but I know your husband, Mark, and I would like to talk to you about him."

Standing with a bag of groceries in one arm, Lindsay said nothing at first.

"Are you there?"

"Yes, I'm here. Who are you?"

"It doesn't matter who I am, does it?"

"Yes, it matters, because without your identifying who you are, I'm not going to talk to you." Silence on the other end and then a click. If she doesn't want to tell me her name, she can go to hell, Lindsay thought as she unpacked the groceries. No one is going to make a mystery call about Mark and then not tell her name, but she knew in her heart, that it was BJA. She must be desperate to resort to anonymous calls. Obviously, Mark isn't playing the game anymore, and it is time to show her power over him by calling his wife.

Lindsay picked up the phone and called Mark's office, but he was in a meeting and would be unreachable all afternoon. Well, it would have to wait until he got home, and then she would tell him her plans. Surprised he would be, but he would know that she meant business this time. She made a wonderful dinner and baked Mark's favorite dessert, apple pie, as she planned her next move. Walking upstairs to put on a very smart outfit from the specialty shop at Saks, Lindsay laughed out loud over the reaction that Mark would have when he heard.

The children and Lindsay ate an early dinner as Mark would be late that night.

"Mom, you look so happy! What happened?"

Jennifer sat at the head of the table in Mark's place, watching her with a strange look on her face. "Mom, come on, are we moving again?"

Matt was as interested as Jennifer. Only Megan didn't ask. After cleaning up from dinner, Lindsay put on some old tapes of the fifties and sixties to hum along with while she folded clothes in the laundry room. The Beatles tape had a tune that reminded Lindsay of Scott, and she smiled at the memory of the phone call earlier. When "Hang on Sloopy" started, Lindsay twisted into the family room and demonstrated for the children. They were hysterical as she did all the steps and hip movements along with singing the words. All of a sudden she felt a tap on her shoulder, and Mark was standing there beaming from ear to ear and, following her lead, they twisted together to the music and the clapping of the children. The old feelings of Mark's arms around her brought back memories that were sweet and wonderful and she felt an inner glow as they danced away the evening together.

Ending the evening with ice cream and pie, they sat on the patio and watched the children take a late night dip in the pool. If it could always be this good, Lindsay would never ask for another thing, but she knew better than to dream again, as it would never happen with Mark.

"Lindsay, tonight when I walked in and saw you dancing, it reminded me of the very first time I saw you at that dance. My heart pounded just like it did that night with wanting you in my arms. I know that you don't always believe me, but I really do love you very much."

Lindsay's heart was breaking, as she heard his words, with wanting to believe him one more time, but the price was too great for the times like this one with all the words she wanted to hear and believe. In his arms, Lindsay felt the stress as he tried to hold on to her.

"Mark, I received a phone call from a woman today." Lindsay felt his arms stiffen as he tried to pull her closer so that she wouldn't push him away with her next words. "Did you hear me?"

Letting his arms drop, he walked back to his chair and sat down. "What did she say?"

"Mark, I didn't talk to her, because she wouldn't identify herself, but I believe that her initials are BJA."

Looking like someone had slapped him, he just stared at her before asking, "How do you know about her initials?"

Lindsay looked at the water in the pool and waited to compose herself.

"I know about the locket you had inscribed at the hotel jewelry store. I've known about her, but I really didn't know much until the other day on the mobile phone and today. Do you want to tell me about her?" Shaking his head no, he walked into the house and up the stairs to their room.

Lindsay heard the sprinklers again that night, not from their room, but from the chaise lounge that she was still sitting in, wondering how everyone would accept her decision tomorrow. She was at a no-return place in her marriage and life, and she was ready to gamble on both of them for the sake of her sanity. Mark found Lindsay in the same place he had left her the night before.

"Lindsay, are you crazy? Have you been outside all night? Come on, Lindsay, we can work through this together, can't we? Please Lindsay, say something. You know that I don't want to lose you or the children."

Turning to face him, Lindsay said the words that she had heard running through her mind all night.

"Mark, I'm taking the children and leaving as soon as I can arrange everything." The words felt like big rocks coming out of her mouth, each word a heavy burden to cast aside.

"Lindsay, are you crazy? You can't do this to me or my career. What will people say?"

"Really, Mark, I'm sure that you will figure out an answer that will save your reputation. You are a very clever man, and I know that you are very good at making up stories, and I'm sure that this one will be spectacular."

Walking upstairs to wake the children for school, Lindsay felt like a robot performing a duty. All the feelings Lindsay had had for Mark were suddenly gone, and an emptiness consumed her body.

After the children left, Lindsay waited to make the arrangements that she needed to make for their new life. The first call was to Smythe Cramer in Hudson to see if they had a rental house for six months so that Matt could graduate with his class and Lindsay could see Mark, Jr. through his hernia surgery. Yes, they had a furnished house that would be ideal. Lindsay took it sight unseen. The next call was to the airlines to figure out a schedule for departure times.

Lindsay dressed and went to the bank and removed ten thousand dollars and had traveler's checks made out to carry with them. She waited in the school office for the girls and then went to Garces and picked up Matt and took them to lunch. Sitting at the Jack in the Box, she told them of her plans to take them back to Hudson.

The plan was met with mixed emotions, sadness at leaving their dad behind and the joy of going home to a place that they loved. After returning them to their schools, Lindsay called Mark and stopped at his office.

"Lindsay, I've been thinking about what you said this morning, and I'll support any decision that you make. In fact, I'll even try to get a transfer back to Atlanta."

"Mark, I need time to sort things out about us, where this marriage is going. I plan to just rest and think while I'm back in Hudson."

Sitting behind his massive desk, Mark tried to look hurt and disappointed, but Lindsay knew that it was an act. His mind was already working on a scheme as they sat. She laughed to herself as she realized how well she read him, and if she controlled her emotions, she could really see him clearly.

"Well, in that case, Lindsay, let me tell you about a plan I have." Lindsay knew it, he had already figured his next move to his best advantage.

"Mark, you are amazing. Even with us leaving, you want to figure out a strategy that will help you."

"No, Lindsay, remember, it is always for us, never just for me."

"Mark, someday it will only be just for you. I know it in my heart."

"Honey, how can you say that? You know that I would never leave you for anyone."

"Mark, you really are a salesman, aren't you?" Almost

out the door, Lindsay paused to look back at Mark. Sitting behind his massive desk, Lindsay could almost see the wheels turning in his mind.

Walking to the plane was like walking the last mile of life. Looking back to where Mark was standing, Lindsay felt as if she was truly a deserter to the cause. Mark stood by the fence as he watched them board; his look was unreadable. Was he sad, or was he just contemplating his next move? How could anyone ever really tell with him? Sitting in a window seat, Lindsay watched him by the fence and cried deep, sad tears of loneliness and disappointment that her life had come to this sad situation.

Something in Lindsay made her get up and run down the steps to where Mark was standing. "Mark, please promise that you will change, and I'll stay and work through this." After begging and pleading for him to change, she waited for his answer.

"Lindsay, you know that none of this is my fault. I'm just a victim of circumstances, and you choose to believe other people and not me. What can I say except that I hope that we'll soon be together in Atlanta. Tell the children that I'm working on being transferred back there." Lindsay knew that Mark would use this situation to his betterment and he did. She walked back to the plane and cried all the way to Cleveland, Ohio, where her parents met them at the airport.

Getting off the plane, the coolness of the early morning was a far cry from the heat of Bakersfield. Looking up at the viewing area, she saw her parents standing at the railing, watching them deplane. Lindsay had come full circle in her life. It had only been a short time since her parents watched them leave for Atlanta, and now they were watching them return without Mark. The happiness of seeing her parents was diminished by the loneliness and emptiness she felt in her heart.

Driving to their new sight-unseen home was a mixture of happiness and sorrow for all of them. They had left, a complete family, and now one member was perhaps gone forever. The road was icy and snowy as they drove to Hudson, but the freshness of freedom from worry and stress made the ride a ride to a new start, beginning with or without Mark.

# Chapter 22

The house was just as the real estate company had said it would be. Walking into someone else's furnished house was a very unnerving feeling. The center hall had a sweeping staircase with white railings that circled the upstairs hallway. Four bedrooms were off the circular hallway with two bathrooms. That night it felt very strange to be sleeping in someone else's bed, and as the night became dawn, Lindsay wondered who might be sleeping in her bed with Mark.

The early morning light showed the first snowstorm of the season; the ground was covered with six inches of snow, and everything looked beautiful and clean. Lindsay heard the children get up just as she put the coffee pot on the stove. The fire in the family room crackled and spouted and made the morning feel snug and cozy as she curled up on the love seat and drank her coffee. Megan came down and ran to the front door to see how deep it was and if she would need boots for the trip into town.

"Mom, I just love being here, but I wish that Dad was here, too. I wish that he had never taken that job, and we had always been here in Hudson. Maggie and I are going to meet under the clock tower, and then we are going to Mary and Ted's for lunch."

Her face radiated as she spoke, and Lindsay knew that

she had made the right decision to bring them back to a place that they loved.

Jennifer came down in her flannel nightgown to see what was going on and to say that her stomach hurt.

"Mom, I loved sleeping here last night. I could hear the wind howl and the sleet against the window panes. I'm glad that Grandma bought us flannel pajamas and flannel sheets. It was so toasty warm all night that I didn't want to wake up this morning and get out of bed."

The phone started ringing. It rang all morning, each of the children hearing from their friends as word got around that the Summerfield children were back in town. The happy voices could be heard throughout the house, and plans were made to meet their friends here and there. The house became quiet as the last one left. Lindsay glanced at the clock and realized that it was eleven o'clock in Bakersfield and she hadn't heard from Mark. She dialed their number, only to get a busy signal, which surprised her, as they had a double line and the call would usually rotate over to the other line. She put the phone down, paced the living room, and watched the snow falling outside. Making a mental note to call the real estate company to see who would plow the driveway, Lindsay tried their number again. This time Mark answered the phone.

"Honey, I was just going to call you. How is everything in Hudson?"

They talked about the kids and the snow and what was in the headlines and then talked about Bakersfield.

"Mark, I hope that I made the right decision."

Being assured that she had, Lindsay felt better and more relaxed with the old Mark on the phone.

"Lindsay, I've written a letter to Champion explaining everything and my desire to return to Atlanta."

"Mark, do you really think that this is what you want?"

"Absolutely, Lindsay, this place is not for me. I want to be back at corporate headquarters."

Feeling relieved, Lindsay asked when he would be back for the holidays.

"Lindsay, I'll check it out and call you in the next day or two with my travel plans."

Hanging up the phone, Lindsay felt as she did before all the moving and stress had entered her life.

Showering, Lindsay felt the hot water against her skin and her nerve endings relaxing. Crawling back into bed, she fell asleep and slept for hours.

Dressed in warm clothes, Lindsay drove into Hudson and window-shopped up and down Main Street. She had forgotten what a beautiful place this area was, with Western Reserve architecture and wonderful gardens and brick side-walks. The gazebo was decorated with greenery and red bows, as were the stores. Walking into Saywell's for a hot chocolate, Lindsay realized what a small-town girl she really was. The fountain and bar stools looked inviting and worn from many years of use; maybe that's what she liked about Hudson—tradition. The same families for generations, with history of a time passed, not a new development with the average house occupancy being five years or less. The kids coming in looked normal in corduroys and sweaters, not high heels and makeup smeared on their face.

"I heard that you were back, Lindsay." It was the pharmacist who had filled so many prescriptions for Lindsay and the family.

"Yes, we are back so that Matt can graduate with his class."

"Sounds like you are a very caring parent. Most parents wouldn't do that for their children."

"I would do anything for my children."

Thinking about what she had just said, she realized that

they were her whole life. Finished with her hot chocolate, she wished everyone a happy holiday and walked over to the library to check out some reading material. The snow and living without Mark would leave her a lot of time on her hands.

The museum had a historical room that housed antique clothes, dolls, as well as furniture and the history of Hudson. Standing in the part that was a reproduction of an eighteenth-century house, Lindsay thought about the first settlers coming this way in a carriage pulled by horses through the snow. Lindsay wondered how it must have been to leave family and friends and move to such a remote area. There had to be great trust in the person that they married. Never would Lindsay have that kind of trust in Mark; he had seen to that with all his escapades. The street lights came on as she drove back to their new home. In the house, she found a houseful of children watching the football game between Ohio State and Michigan She said hello to all and walked upstairs to the master bedrroom and lay down on top of the comforter and pulled an afghan over herself and fell asleep.

"Mom, Dad is on the phone. He's at the airport and wants you to pick him up." Megan was so excited as she shook her awake. "Mom, I knew he would come and stay with us. Didn't I tell you that he loves us?"

By now, Matt and Jennifer were sitting on Lindsay's bed with the portable phone in Matt's hand. "Mark, what a surprise. I thought you were going to wait a few days and then call."

"Honey, I woke up to an empty house, and I couldn't stand it, so here I am. Come get me." Lindsay found out exactly where to meet him and drove to the Cleveland airport.

Seeing Mark standing at the American baggage area brought a smile to her face. She had missed him far more than she thought she would in such a short time.

"Lindsay, I'm so glad to see you!" and with that, she was in his arms, feeling his kisses and warm body next to hers as the snow covered the windshield.

The drive back to Hudson was like going down memory lane as they talked about how happy they had been there as a family. Matt, Megan, and Jennifer were waiting in the doorway with all the outside lights on. Mark, Jr. would be home that night, and they would be a complete family for the first time in a long time.

"Dad, come see our new home." Megan was so pleased that she had been able to have the best bedroom in the house. Matt and Jennifer had chosen the smaller rooms, which were on each side of the master bedroom.

The children's friends stopped in to say hello to Mark. They listened to the children's happy voices as they made plans to go out for the many parties that were scheduled for the evening. Mark and Lindsay curled up on the couch and watched the Saturday night movie while they waited for Mark, Jr. to arrive from Columbus. The fire roared as Mark put on new logs and sipped hot apple cider with rum. Hearing a car in the driveway, they opened the door to find their eldest child standing in the dark with a smile on his face. They hugged him together, and in her heart, Lindsay felt the first true feeling of happiness in such a very long time. As long as they were together, all was well with the world.

Climbing the stairs to a strange bed, Lindsay walked arm in arm with Mark, feeling safe and secure. Lying in his arms, she listened for the children to come home from their parties. Mark, Jr. was asleep in Matt's room, warm and safe with his family, who loved and cared about him. On Monday, he would have surgery, and Lindsay would be there to take care of him, not a stranger in a strange hospital. Yes, it was worth all this to see her family together again.

# Chapter 23

Waking early the next morning, Mark and Lindsay lay in bed listening to the howling of the wind outside. The furnace had been running constantly all night, so they both knew that the temperature had dropped drastically below the freezing mark. The frosted window panes were covered with beautiful ice designs. Remembering how her mother would say that Jack Frost had visited them when their kitchen window panes were covered with frost brought a smile to her face. Lindsay's mother and dad had always made sure that her brother and she were very secure and happy, and memories of those happy times ran through her mind. If the roads cleared up, they would be here for dinner, and they would enjoy stories of when the children were young, and more importantly, they would be together again.

"Lindsay, I could lie here all day next to you." Reaching over, he brought her to him, and they snuggled together under the worn coverlet that was quilted with tiny hand-made stitches. Someone had worked very hard on the quilt, and Lindsay wondered why the Thompsons had left it behind.

"Mark, I wish that we could be snowed in for about a year and no one would have to leave."

She kissed Mark on the nose and slid out of bed and

went into the bathroom. Looking out from a tiny space that was not frosted, Lindsay saw the damage of the night before and knew that her parents would not arrive for dinner that afternoon. The street was covered with at least eight inches of snow; it was obvious that no one would be able to drive on it until the plows came by.

"Guess what, Mark?"

"We're snowed in."

"You win the sixty-four-thousand-dollar prize."

"Lindsay, I have all the prizes I want in this house."

"Mark, you always know the right thing to say, don't you?"

"Honey, I mean what I say, and I mean this."

"I'd really like to believe that, but I wonder why you can't stop getting into compromising positions that seem to only hurt me and the children."

"Honey, I told you before that it's over with her, and I don't want to talk about it again. Please, let's not ruin the time we are having with all the children together."

"I want it to stop, Mark."

"I know, I know, Lindsay, but I am only a victim of that crazy woman."

"Mark, she wouldn't expect anything if you didn't show her that you were willing."

"Come here and let me show you how willing I can be." Covering them totally with the quilt, Mark began kissing Lindsay's forehead and stroking her back. "Lindsay, let's make this a Christmas that the children will never forget."

Lindsay really wanted nothing more than that for everyone. Mark was tender and loving as they made love that morning while the children slept peacefully and safely in their bedrooms. Lying together, Lindsay heard the sound of the house waking up to movement of the children as they made their breakfast downstairs.

"Lindsay, let's go down and have breakfast with the children. I want to tell them about the plans for Christmas and New Year's Eve.

"Mark, only promise what you can do and nothing else."

"Honey, you know me better than that." Looking disappointed, Mark put on his robe and slippers and went down to see the children.

Lindsay lay in the middle of the bed and felt the warmth of his body still on the sheets. The pillow case had the aroma of his aftershave. She pressed her face into the pillowcase and felt his arms around her again. Hearing Mark call her from downstairs, Lindsay got out of bed and put on her robe and slippers and went down to the dining room, where everyone was waiting for her to start breakfast.

While beating the waffle mix, Lindsay heard Mark talk to the boys about school and sports and heard the chatter of the girls as they talked about the party the night before. She smiled at how happy their "new" home sounded after so many months of unhappiness in Bakersfield.

"Mom, why are you smiling?" It was Mark, Jr. standing next to her at the stove.

"Mark, I'm so happy to see my family together and especially you, honey." She threw her arms around him. Lindsay felt her firstborn in her arms again just as he had been nineteen years ago on that cold October morning so long ago. He was safe in her arms again, and she held him tightly, never wanting him to leave her side again.

"Lindsay, hurry up with breakfast; we have to buy the tree today."

Conversation on what kind, how big, and where they would put the tree took up the breakfast table talk. Thinking of what she would decorate the tree with, Lindsay thought of all the Christmas ornaments in her grandmother's attic; she decided to drive into Cleveland and borrow the ornaments while she was in the nursing home. At least they could get the tree up and the lights on while everyone was willing to help.

The snow plow came down the street just as Mark and the boys finished shoveling the steps and sidewalk.

"Lindsay, come on; it's time to get the tree." Piled into the car with the ax and saw, they drove to Peninsula to their favorite Christmas tree farm to select their tree.

The roads were barely passable as they sang Christmas carols on the ride to the farm. The farm was open, but they were the only car in the parking lot; the owner greeted them with cheers of being brave enough to venture out in the snow.

"I was wondering if you would be back this year or not."

"Mr. Primrose, is there anyone else who has prettier trees than you do?"

"Mrs. Summerfield, you always know the way to my heart."

"Well, I hope your heart is big enough to give us a sleigh ride around the farm, as it is too deep to walk through the snow."

"It will be my pleasure, but let me get some hot cider for the ride. Mrs. Primrose just made a gallon of it just in case, and I know that she will be happy to supply a thermos for all of us to take on our hunt for that perfect tree."

With a wink he disappeared into the farm house, and as they waited, they jumped up and down trying to keep warm. On his return, they piled into a very old sleigh and began their journey for the perfect tree.

Singing "Jingle Bells" and "Rudolph the Red Nosed Reindeer," they went up one hill and down another until they came to a grove of beautiful blue spruces about twelve feet high and beautifully shaped, and they knew that they had found the perfect place to find their tree. The debate over which one to buy was comical as each child had their hands on a tree of their choice, including Mark. Standing in the newly falling snow, they debated about each one's choice until they were down to a choice between Mark's tree and Megan's tree. The group decided to flip a coin, as both trees were beautiful. Mr. Primrose was in charge of the coin flip. Lindsay didn't know which one would win as both stood silently waiting. Putting her hand on Mr. Primrose's arm, Lindsay said, "We'll take both of them." Mark and Megan both could not stop smiling as they loaded the trees on the roof of the car.

"Lindsay, what are we going to do with two trees?"

"Mark, we'll put one in the family room and one in the living room."

"Honey, what a nice idea. You are wonderful."

"We'll have to buy lights on the way home and ribbon and candy canes. This tree is going to be very unadorned and beautiful."

"Mom, can we hang popcorn on the tree, and cranberries?" Jennifer was disappointed that her tree had not been the one chosen, but Lindsay knew that she would be happy making bows for the tree.

"Jennifer, you can pick out the ribbon for the bows and the candy canes.

Smiling, Lindsay looked back at her face and saw the yellow glow to her skin, and the smile faded from her face. Tomorrow, she would call the Cleveland Clinic and make an appointment for a medical workup for Jennifer. She had to keep a close eye on her. She was reminded that there was no better place than the clinic to take her.

Matt and Mark talked about the football game between the Browns and the Bears that afternoon and which one would win the game.

"Lindsay, don't forget that we have to watch the game

while the trees thaw out." Smiling, he reached out for her hand and held it all the way home.

Was this a man who didn't love his wife, or did he have multiple personalities that only a psychiatrist could decipher? A psychiatrist—. . . Scott. How had Lindsay forgotten about his comments in so short a time? All Mark had to do was show her what she wanted to see, and she was his to control and manipulate.

Home after stopping at Ace Hardware for two tree stands and the ribbon and the candy canes at Acme, they took off their winter coats and gloves and settled down to soup and ham sandwiches with hot apple cider in front of the television set to watch the football games. Half the room was for the Browns, and the other half was for the Bears. Her parents arrived at half time and were greeted with hugs and kisses as the boys took their coats.

"Lindsay, the roads were terrible. I told your dad to turn back many times, but he wanted to see the kids. He has really missed them."

Lindsay's mother sat on the kitchen chair with a cup of coffee as they made up for lost time gossiping about friends and neighbors. It felt so good to sit and visit without having to make a long distance call.

"Dad looks well; how are you doing?"

"Fine, now that you are back for awhile." Hearing the boys call for more Cokes and chips, they went in to join them.

Megan and Jennifer set the table while Lindsay sliced the roast beef and dished out the vegetables. Mom had brought homemade bread and a chocolate cake from Hough's bakery, Lindsay's favorite. Sitting at the dining room table with candlelight and the snow falling outside, peaceful was the only word Lindsay could think of for how she felt, totally peaceful.

Mark, Jr. went upstairs to take the medicated shower

that was needed before his hernia surgery in the morning. Lindsay was relieved that Mark would be able to drive them to the hospital and be with her. Her parents decided to spend the night and go to the hospital with them, too. Mark and Lindsay watched the evening movie from their bed. Tired and happy from all the excitement, she fell asleep before the movie was over. The warmth of Mark next to her was all she needed to feel secure; that night she dreamed of Scott.

"Lindsay, Lindsay, where are you?" Lindsay could hear Scott's voice, but she couldn't see him in the dense fog.

"Scott, here I am, over here behind the doorway. Can't you see me?"

"Lindsay, I told you to be careful where Mark is concerned, and you aren't listening to my warning."

"Scott, Mark is being good, can't you see how good he's been?"

"Come closer to me, Lindsay, so that I can tell you more."

"I can't find you in the fog. Please come to me."

"The fog is too thick, Lindsay, and I can't see you, but I tell you that you are being very naive, and your judgment is clouded by your love for him."

"Scott, what are you talking about?"

"Didn't Mark tell you about—"

Waking up with a start, Lindsay sat straight up in bed and looked around for Scott in the darkness and wondered if she had been dreaming or if Scott had come to her. What had Scott meant? Pulling herself together, she looked over at Mark sound asleep in the same position as when he had fallen asleep. Talking to herself, Lindsay walked down the steps in the dark with the wonderful pine smell from the trees enveloping the house. The two trees looked naked and vulnerable as they stood unadorned in the Christmas tree stands, waiting to be decorated in the morning. The soft pine needles fell silently to the floor as Lindsay touched the branches and thought how similar the trees were to her marriage to Mark, beautiful when adored and vulnerable when abandoned.

Snow fell outside as Lindsay watched the snow plows clear the roads, and Scott's warning came back to her over and over. What had Scott tried to tell her, or was it just her insecurity playing tricks on her again?

Walking back upstairs, Lindsay looked into each child's room and marveled at the wonderful human creations that they had created with their love for each other.

Lying in bed, Lindsay felt Mark stirring; she reached for his hand and felt the softness of his skin against hers and knew that no matter what he did, she would never leave him until she was sure that she no longer could go on with their marriage.

Turning over to her side of the bed, Lindsay felt Mark nuzzle against her neck, and all the fears and questions of her dream were put out of her mind as she lay in the quiet of their bedroom listening to Mark's breathing against her neck.

# Chapter 24

Driving to the hospital in the early morning light, Lindsay was relieved that Mark was with them, but the dream she had last night haunted her. What had the dream meant? Was it just her insecurity about Mark and their life together that always made her look for the dark side instead of the sunny side of life? Mark's constant ups and downs had put her on a merry-go-round, and she never knew when it would stop and whether she would fall off when it did stop.

Akron City Hospital was in full swing when they registered at the outpatient surgery desk. Mark gave all the information to the admitting clerk while Mark, Jr. and Lindsay sat in silence. Mark, Jr. was so scared that Lindsay hoped they would not have to wait long for his operation. Mark returned with the consent forms for Mark, Jr. to sign and for his bracelet.

"Mark, don't worry; we'll be right here, and we'll see you soon in recovery. I'm so glad that I was able to be here."

Smiling up at his dad, Mark, Jr. said, "I'm glad too, Dad. I've missed you and Mom and the kids."

"Mom, don't forget to call Kim when the surgery is over and let her know how everything went."

Kim was Mark, Jr.'s girlfriend from high school, and

they were like two peas in a pod with similar likes and dislikes, a perfect pair.

"Don't worry, I'll call Kim, and I'm sure that she will be over tonight to see you."

Just then the orderly came for Mark, Jr., and they walked to the outpatient surgery door with him and kissed him and wished him well. Tears were in Lindsay's eyes as she watched him look back at her and smile slightly. His big dark brown eyes reminded her of when he was a little boy, so sweet and loving all the time, so much like her side of the family, not in the least like Rebecca. Rebecca, would not have even been here for Mark or his sisters or brother. Mark had come a long way in adapting to her caring family's ways, but there still were times that the emotional scars of his child-hood surfaced, and they would be abandoned for the current fun thing or place just as Rebecca did with him. Lindsay still cried when she thought of the stories that Mark told about not being cuddled or loved by her, only tolerated because he resembled his dead father so much in looks.

The Stanford sisters, as they were called in the Toledo area, Allison, Elizabeth, and Rebecca, clones all dressed alike with convent type education and discipline. All the sisters had problems with their offspring and seemed to not know why, but Lindsay knew that they had raised their children with the same Victorian rules that they had been raised—"a child should be seen and not heard."

Lindsay thanked God every day that Mark had allowed her to care for her children in the same manner she had been raised, with love and affection.

"Lindsay, a penny for your thoughts." Mark was walking next to Lindsay as he reached for her hand and smiled.

In the coffee shop, they ordered coffee and bagels, which she only nibbled at while all the time her mind was on her son. Would he be all right? Even now, you hear about a simple surgery that went bad and the patient dies or is a vegetable. Please God, don't send that to her, she said as she prayed that Mark, Jr. would be all right.

The Summerfields were called by the volunteer at the front desk of the waiting room. "Mr. and Mrs. Summerfield, your son is in recovery, and the doctor will be right in." They thanked her and returned to their seats, and Lindsay thanked God that he had made it through the surgery.

"Lindsay, Mark, all went well, and you can take him home after his vital signs are stable."

Thanking Dr. Curtis, they felt as if a tremendous load had been lifted from them.

Mark went to the pay phone and called his office. Even from the distance Lindsay was from him, she could see that he was very irritated, as his jaw was twitching and he was grasping his hands as he spoke.

Lindsay slowly walked up behind him and heard him tell Mary, his secretary, "I understand and I'll definitely take care of the situation when I get back to the office. She wants to sell me an insurance policy, and she won't take no for an answer."

Lindsay's whole body trembled with what she now knew to be a major problem for them; BJA was back in the picture and it was the beginning of a fatal attraction for Mark. Mark had not taken care of the situation as he had promised he would, and now she was a thorn in his side to deal with. Feeling the old anger well up inside, Lindsay turned and walked back to her chair and watched Mark talking on the phone and wondered why he had to bring chaos into their lives. Wasn't she enough for him?

Hanging up the phone, Mark just stared at the receiver. He approached the desk and spoke to the volunteer, then walked out of the room. Lindsay watched with interest where he was going, when the volunteer came up to tell her that Mark would be right back and to wait for him there. Thanking her, Lindsay waited until the volunteer became involved with another patient, then she walked in the same direction as Mark had walked. Where was he and why didn't he himself tell her where he was going?

Walking down a deserted hallway, Lindsay heard Mark before she saw him. "Listen, BJ, I don't care what you say; I'm staying with my wife. Don't ever threaten me again, or else you'll regret it."

Mark was screaming as he spoke, and his facial muscles were contorting in spasms. Whatever she was saying was making him furious, and he now paced back and forth.

"I know what I said, but you misunderstood what I meant that weekend in the wine country. All that wine sampling kept me drunk the whole weekend."

Lindsay could hear her voice, but she couldn't make out what she was saying. "Don't call me anymore at the office. I'll call you. Of course I miss you, and I will call you soon."

He hung up and rested his head against the pay phone and just stood there breathing heavily. Turning, he came face to face with Lindsay. Shock was all over his face as he realized that she had heard the conversation.

"Honey, when did you get here?" Walking towards her, he tried to grab her into his arms.

"Don't, Mark."

Trying to break away without making a scene was impossible, as Dr. Curtis came down the hall to walk them back to the recovery room.

"Mark and Lindsay, you two are my favorite patients. I see so many unhappy marriages that when I see you two, I feel that all is well with family life." Lindsay barely saw the floor as the three of them walked together into the recovery room.

Mark, Jr., lying so still and pale against the stark white

sheets, barely opened his eyes as Dr. Curtis spoke to him. "Mark, wake up."

"Hi, Mom and Dad. I'm so glad that you two are here. I really have missed both of you." Slowly his eyes closed and he drifted off to sleep again.

"Lindsay, it will be several hours before Mark will be awake enough to go home, so why don't you two join me for lunch at Rays on the River, and then I'll come back and check Mark again. I'll just leave my number with the recovery nurse and then we'll be off." Without waiting for their answer, he walked away.

Mark seemed relieved that Lindsay would not be able to discuss the phone call until later, and by then they would be home with Mark, Jr., and he knew that she would not make a scene after the surgery. Yes, Mark had a reprieve again, at least until tonight when they would be alone in their bedroom.

The lunch seemed to last forever as Mark and Dr. Curtis talked about everything from golf to politics. Barely touching her shrimp salad, Lindsay toyed with her food until the waiter removed her plate and brought the dessert that Mark had ordered for her. The chocolate mousse was so rich, she felt that she was going to be sick.

"Mark, I know how much you like chocolate mousse. Why don't you take some of mine?"

Mark, thinking that all was well because Lindsay was speaking to him, smiled and took most of the mousse.

Smiling back at him, Lindsay said, "I really think we should get back to the hospital and check on our son, don't you?"

Mark agreed, and they all left together and rode back to the hospital in the newly falling snow.

Reaching the hospital, Lindsay turned to Mark and suggested that he wait at the emergency entrance in case

Mark, Jr. was ready to be discharged, he would then have a warm car waiting for him. Mark seemed to agree and waited while Dr. Curtis and Lindsay walked on together. Mark and Lindsay each needed space from each other to regroup and put on the happy face they needed for the sake of the children and her parents.

Finding Mark, Jr. dressed and alert, Lindsay kissed him and put her arms around him and hugged him to her. "I love you, Markie, always remember that." She felt him relax in her arms and knew that she would never use her anger toward Mark to make her son unhappy and insecure again.

Mark helped his son into the car and covered him with the blanket that they had brought from home just for this purpose. The roads had turned to ice, and the drive home was hazardous and very unnerving, so they rode in silence, neither one taking their eyes off the road.

Lindsay's mom and dad met them at the inside of the garage door as they pulled in. They helped carry Mark, Jr. into the house, as he had fallen back to sleep. Lindsay's mom had made a bed for Mark, Jr. on the living room couch. He slept the rest of the afternoon and into the evening. The dinner her mom had prepared for all of them was delicious and one of Lindsay's favorites, stuffed pork chops, but she was unable to eat more than a couple of bites.

"Lindsay, are you all right?" She had put her hand on Lindsay's and held it while she looked at her.

"Mom, I'm just tired from all the stress and worry."

With that, Lindsay broke into tears and left the table. No one said a word, as if they were in shock, as Lindsay ran up the stairs to her room and lay on her bed and sobbed. The dream had come true, and Scott's warning ran through her mind over and over again, and she cried harder with each thought.

The house was very quiet when Lindsay finally composed herself enough to shower and put on fresh make-up. Walking down the stairs she heard the children talking to Mark, Jr.

"Isn't it great that we are all going to be together for Christmas? Mom and Dad seem so happy that I know that it is going to be a great Christmas."

Lots of talk among them about what they would like for Christmas. Their happy voices only made her sadder as she thought of what had happened earlier at the hospital and what recourse she had. If she took a stand, she would only hurt the children and their Christmas Day; if she didn't, Mark had won again. Who would she sacrifice, herself for them or them for herself?

Taking a deep breath, she walked into the living room and joined in their conversation, putting Mark and BJA out of her mind but not out of her heart. Lindsay's heart was broken beyond repair, and the ache was overwhelming.

# Chapter 25

What is it about Christmas morning that brings out the child in all of us? The first ray of light brought all four children to Lindsay and Mark's bedroom door with wishes of Merry Christmas and urgent messages to hurry up and wake up so that they could open their presents. The magical innocence in each of their faces only brought back memories of the earlier Christmas Days that Lindsay had with Mark and the children.

Remembering their very first Christmas brought a smile to Lindsay's face as she remembered how they had shopped with such care for the perfect tree, only to bring home a tree that was five feet too tall for their little apartment ceiling. The top of the tree was sawed off, and they decorated the remaining bush-shaped tree with Christmas lights. Mark and Lindsay bought their first strand of lights together, not realizing that they had bought a strand of one hundred and forty-five lights, all on one strand, so that each time Mark stepped over the lights, he stepped on a light bulb and caused a horrible popping sound, bringing the people from downstairs up to see if a gun was going off. That Christmas was forever a picture in her mind as one of their happiest, as it was just the two of them together, not needing anyone else but each other. How she wished that Mark still felt that way.

Lindsay and Mark had not spoken at all that previous night, but now they would have to or ruin the day.

"Mom, Dad, come and get your presents." Four happy faces watched as they entered the room. The night before, as was their custom, Lindsay had prepared a table with juice glasses, coffee mugs, and plates so that they could nibble while they opened their gifts. The Christmas holly pattern by Lenox looked beautiful with greenery and candles lit on the linen luncheon cloth. After bringing in the coffee cake, juice, and hot chocolate and coffee, they proceeded to open their presents.

The girls loved their outfits, jewelry, and perfume, and the boys were excited over the new CCA hockey skates and sweaters, Docker pants, and winter jackets. The stockings hung by the fireplace were the last to be opened, and everyone enjoyed the wonderful fun things inside. Turning to Lindsay, Mark said, "Lindsay, I have a special present for you." He handed her a beautifully wrapped gold box. Lindsay saw that it was from Tiffany's; she knew that it was something that would take her breath away.

"Hurry up, Mom, open it."

All four children sat and watched as Lindsay carefully unwrapped the box. The blue felt box was long and narrow, and when she opened it, there was the most beautiful diamond bracelet with twenty ruby hearts spaced among the diamonds. On the card, "A heart for every year that we have been together."

Feeling the tears well up, Lindsay was barely able to contain her feelings as Mark came over and kissed her.

"Merry Christmas, honey, I love you."

The Summerfields sat together in the living room and waited for Lindsay's parents to wake up so that they could open their presents and they theirs. The morning was wonderful with all the excitement that children can bring to

Christmas. The phone was beginning to ring off the hook with the children's friends calling to tell what they got for Christmas and hear what the children had received.

The happy sounds only made Lindsay accept the decision that she had made not to cause a scene about the phone call, but it was a hollow victory for Mark, because this time, Lindsay would not accept that he had been a victim of circumstances. How could he take her to a chalet in the wine country and spend the weekend with her? How could he promise to call her and tell her that he missed her and say it so convincingly that even Lindsay believed that he would the first chance he got?

Touching her bracelet, Lindsay fingered each ruby heart and thought that she had truly earned each one with each forgiveness to Mark. The diamonds sparkled brilliantly. She wondered how he had thought to design such a beautiful bracelet, when she felt his arms around her waist and his nuzzling her neck with his lips.

"Honey, please stick with me, and you'll see how much I really love you and only you." His warm lips kissed her neck, and finally, he turned her around and hungrily kissed her mouth and throat.

"Mark, this is one time that you can't say you were a victim. I heard you on the phone."

Mark's kisses cut off Lindsay's words as he backed her into a corner of the living room and his kisses became more suggestive and erotic until she was sure that he would make passionate love to her in front of everyone.

"Mark, the children . . . my parents . . . this has got to stop."

"Honey, I want you now more than I've ever wanted you."

Mark's erection was very obvious by now, and Lindsay

knew that it would be only a few minutes before someone came into the living room.

"Mark, let's go upstairs, and we'll get dressed."

Mark took it as a sign that they would continue upstairs what had begun downstairs.

"Lindsay, I love you, and you know that this has been one of our happiest Christmases. Don't ruin it."

His hand reached under her robe as they walked upstairs, and the warmth of his hand against her leg only weakened her resolve to refuse his love-making.

"Mark, we have to talk first."

"I am talking. With my hands. Can't you tell?"

"Mark, come on. You know what I mean."

"Lindsay, you love it, I know."

Reaching behind him, he locked the bedroom door, then pushed her back against the bed and straddled her body with his. Slowly he began to unbutton her robe, all the while kissing her with his lips and then his tongue until Lindsay wanted more and more of him. After what seemed a very long time he removed her robe and nightgown and then his own clothes slowly, very slowly, all the time never taking his eyes off her. His body was as lean as it had been the first time she saw him in college, and Lindsay marveled at his muscular body.

"Lindsay, let me show you how much I love you." His lips were hot against hers, and his hardness was moving urgently against her stomach. She felt the warmth between her legs and knew that if she stayed one more minute, she would lose all will power to stop him.

A rap at the door brought both of them to attention.

"Yes, what is it? Mom and I are getting dressed."

"Dad, there is a lady on the phone that will not leave her name or a message." It was Megan. "She called three times already."

Why hadn't Lindsay heard the phone? Picking up the phone, she saw that the ringer had been turned off.

"Mark, did you turn off the ringer?"

The look on his face told her he had.

"Never mind, Megan, I'll take care of this." With that, Lindsay picked up the phone. "Hello, this is Mrs. Summerfield. What do you want?"

There was silence on the other end; then the person spoke. "I want to talk to Mark."

"I'm sorry, but Mark is not taking any calls today, as it is a family day. You will have to call him at the office."

How Lindsay had thought of that reply, she did not know, but she was worried that one of the children was on the extension phone, and she didn't want them to hear the conversation.

"I need to talk to him. He promised that he would call me, and I'm all alone on Christmas Day."

Lindsay wanted to reach out and hit her through the phone and then Mark after her.

"Sorry, but until you find someone who is available, it will always be lonely for you."

No longer was any feeling inside her for herself or for Mark, only an emptiness. All feelings for Mark had suddenly left her as she replaced the phone and walked to the bathroom to take a shower. Mark sat naked on the bed, staring at her as she walked by him.

Turning to him, Lindsay said, "I told you never to bring that sort of thing into my home or to my children. Next time, I'll leave you."

The bathroom door did not have a lock on it, but Lindsay felt sure that Mark would not bother her. She ran the shower and stepped into the hot water. She let the water massage her tired body as she leaned against the wall. She didn't hear Mark come in, but she felt his presence. Suddenly the shower door opened, and Mark joined her in the shower. Grabbing her hands behind her, he held her body against the wall and pressed his body against hers.

"Tell me again. How are you going to leave me? Are you going to throw me out or take me to the cleaners in court? Well, let me tell you one thing. I'm still your husband, and I have rights, so whether you like it or not, I'm going to make love to you now."

His hands held her where he wanted her as his body took what it wanted from her. His strength was overwhelming, and Lindsay knew that she could do nothing to stop him but scream, and that was the one thing he knew that she wouldn't do with everyone in the house. His lovemaking was like something she had never experienced before, no tenderness, only rough sex.

"Stop, please stop." Lindsay's words fell on deaf ears as he continued taking her.

"Lindsay, this is how I treat the women I meet. Is this what you want, or do you want love the way you have known it to be?"

Lindsay said nothing and let him finish. When he was through, Lindsay looked directly at him and said, "If you ever do that again I will make you the sorriest man in the world."

Stepping around him, she got out of the shower and dressed. Walking into the kitchen, Lindsay found that the standing rib roast was already in the oven and the children watching a football game. No one had missed Lindsay and Mark, but the dull ache that had begun to penetrate her every muscle reminded her of what had happened upstairs.

"What's for dinner?" It was Mark, all dressed and happy as can be.

"Mark, Lindsay bought a beautiful rib roast, and it should be ready around five."

Lindsay's mom seemed not to notice anything and proceeded to peel potatoes. Soon Lindsay heard the sounds of children talking to their dad and grandfather in the next room. Everyone was happy but Lindsay; she had no choice except to put on an act for all of them.

The afternoon and evening seemed to last forever as Lindsay waited for her parents to leave and the children to go to bed. Mark never mentioned what had happened upstairs or on the phone. He was full of compliments on this wonderful day and after the beautiful dinner. An outsider looking in would have thought that this was a picture-perfect family. The fine cracks were widening in the picture-perfect family, and it scared Lindsay more than she wanted to believe or accept.

Watching Mark pack his clothes only made Lindsay want to tell him to stay, that they could work things out again, but she knew that it was too late to try to save whatever was left of their marriage.

The children had returned to school, and it was just Mark and Lindsay alone in the house. Mark walked over to her side of the bed and sat down and looked at her.

"Lindsay, I want to thank you for not ruining the holiday for the children and me. I know that you get horribly hurt by my actions, and I'm sorry for that, but I just don't mean to hurt you, and in the end I do." Taking her hand in his, he held it tightly against his heart before he spoke again. "I feel so awful that I don't have your trust and love anymore, and I wonder sometimes why I work as hard as I do to provide a home and lifestyle that I enjoy only when I feel like it. I don't want you to take my indiscretions lightly, but I really don't understand why I do it, except that I was raised by a grandfather who had many affairs in my presence. My mom didn't even love me."

Tears were flowing down his face as he spoke and Lindsay's heart broke as she watched him bare his soul.

Reaching up to him, Lindsay held him in her arms as he sobbed uncontrollably. She cried with him as she would for a child of her own. Mark had become her child, and she hadn't realized it until now. Hadn't Lindsay always taken care of him and protected him from all the painful events, including his own mother, Rebecca? Holding him like this, Lindsay wondered how often he, as a child, had cried himself to sleep, unloved and unwanted.

How could Lindsay turn her back on him and leave her children fatherless in this mean, cold world? Would she ever love someone like she loved Mark? She held him closer to her and rocked him back and forth as one would a baby.

"Please, Lindsay, one more chance, and I promise that you will never regret it. I promise that I will be faithful and true for the rest of our lives together." How much Lindsay wanted to believe him and trust in him again, but could she? "If you will just think about it and tell me your decision when I call you tonight, I would be ever so grateful, and if your decision is to leave me, then I will have to accept that and somehow go on without you and the children. I was raised without a father, and I know what kind of pain that is, so please, carefully consider all your options."

Driving Mark to the airport, Lindsay barely said a word. Mark kept asking her not to throw away twenty years but to reconsider with her heart, not her head.

Lindsay watched Mark walk through the glass doors at Cleveland's Hopkins Airport, and she felt as if a part of her had died. She felt so sad and lonely. Mark would be calling tonight for an answer, and she would have to be ready to give him one.

Crying all the way home, Lindsay knew what the decision would be, and the tears were for her pain, not his.

515
185
85
99

700
184
——
884

850